Dead Scare

DAVID DEMELLO

Outskirts Press, Inc.
Denver, Colorado

Dead Scare
All Rights Reserved
Copyright © 2006 David DeMello

Outskirts Press
http://www.outskirtspress.com

ISBN-10: 1-59800-919-2
ISBN-13: 978-1-59800-919-4

Outskirts Press and the "OP" logo are trademarks belonging to
Outskirts Press, Inc.

Printed in the United States of America

*To my family,
especially my parents;
the biggest fans I will ever have.
I love you all.*

Chapter 1

Dr. Philip Nickerson shifted in his black leather chair trying to get comfortable. "So tell me, Fred; since your last appointment with me have your panic attacks gotten any better?"

Fred looked back at Nickerson, but did not respond. He had so much to tell; yet he didn't know where to begin.

"Fred," Nickerson began, "it's very important that you tell me everything that comes to you. I am here to help you. I *want* to help you. Panic attacks are very common. Especially with young men like yourself. You're in school, you have a lot of stress, and I'm sure a heavy workload. And besides college, you also have your home life and your job. Stress can cause panic attacks. I'm here to help you figure out what truly is causing you the stress." Nickerson was speaking quickly. "If we minimize what you are stressing about, what you fear, then we will minimize your attacks. I promise you, Fred, one day they may not even exist anymore. But you've got to work with me here. Let's work together to figure this out. You don't want to keep seeing me every week, do you? I'm sure you have better things to do than spend an hour of your life with an old man like me, huh?"

Fred spoke slowly, "I so badly want to get rid of them. I really do."

Nickerson could see how fragile Fred's mind was. He seemed desperate. He wanted to relieve whatever pressure was causing his attacks.

Nickerson removed his glasses and set them on his desk. Fred glared into the deep-set brown eyes that loomed before him. "I need your help, Dr. Nickerson. I want to be able to live a life without worrying when they'll strike again."

"I know you do. We all do. That's what I'm here for, Fred. I'm here to help you. We all must conquer our fears. Your attacks are brought on by fear, Fred, but once you learn to conquer them they will not haunt you any longer," Nickerson responded. "Once you forget about them, you will be okay. The more you think about getting panic attacks, the better the chance they will occur."

"I cannot learn to conquer them if I do not know what I have to conquer!" Fred shouted.

Nickerson was taken aback. "Calm down. No need to shout. We'll figure it out. We will."

Fred dropped his head and stared at the floor. "That's what you told me last week. They've gotten worse since then. I want them gone," he said. "I want them gone!"

"It takes time. Everything takes time. Things don't just disappear over night."

Fred slowly picked up his head and stopped when

he had made eye contact with Nickerson. "Will they ever disappear?"

Nickerson didn't know for sure, but he couldn't tell Fred that. "Of course they will. Give it time. Last week you told me you were okay. What happened in a week? You seemed all enthusiastic that Spring Break was coming up. When that comes around you should have less worries than ever. What has happened in the past week?"

"Too much." It was all he could muster.

Nickerson's eyebrows lowered. "What do you mean? When was the last time you felt a panic attack coming on?"

"Remember how I told you about that Abnormal Psychology class I'm taking?" Fred asked.

"Yes. What about it?"

"Well last week, maybe a few days after my appointment with you, we got our first test handed back," Fred said, rubbing his forehead.

Nickerson was interested. "And this was when you started having one?"

"Yes. I got all sweaty, and my heart started beating faster, and I was dizzy, and nervous, and scared..." Fred had to stop. It was bringing back a bad memory.

"Take your time. Tell me as much as you can. What were you afraid of?" Nickerson asked.

"I don't know. It happens to me a lot when tests are being handed back. I just stress out. I feel sick." Fred shook his head. "I become afraid."

"Afraid of what, Fred? What are you afraid of? That you didn't do well? That you failed?" Nickerson questioned with a grimace.

"I guess so. Then the professor tells how well the

class did and how many people did bad and how many people did well. There's thirty-five people in the class and I think only seven passed." Fred was trembling.

"So it's a difficult class. It's normal to be afraid of failing. If only seven people passed then it's probably more the professor's fault than the students'. People fail all the time." Nickerson stopped for a brief moment and rubbed his forehead. "And they just get back up and try again. They shake it off. Fred, if the only thing that brings on panic attacks is a failing test grade, you shouldn't have much to worry about." Nickerson tried to reason with him.

"That's just the thing. I didn't fail. I got an 'A.'"

Nickerson looked directly into Fred's eyes. "Well congratulations. So what was the problem then?"

Fred ignored the question. "I have never received a grade lower than a B on anything. Never throughout grammar school or High school, not even since I began college. I'm basically a straight 'A' student. I have yet to fail at anything."

Nickerson grabbed his glasses off the desk and put them back on. "Well, there you go, that may be the problem."

Fred didn't understand. "What do you mean? Me not failing is why I panic?"

"In a way, yes. People tend to fear most what they do not know. If you do not know what it is like to fail you will always stress out about even the slightest thought of failure." Nickerson closed his eyes tightly. It was as if he was fighting back something. He opened them again and shook his head. "People who fear things cannot grasp the idea of life without fear. In a way fear feeds them. It makes them do things they do, and not do

4

things they don't do. But once you conquer what you fear, it will no longer exist," Nickerson answered.

"So the only way I can get rid of my panic attacks is if I let myself fail?"

Nickerson nodded. "I don't want you to go and intentionally try to fail a test, that wouldn't do anything. You need to fail at something on your own. Do you like sports?"

"Some," Fred answered.

"What kinds?"

"Baseball and football, mostly."

"Okay. What about basketball? Do you like basketball? Or soccer even?"

"Not really. I'm not very good at either of them," Fred replied.

"Well there you go."

"What do you mean?" Fred asked.

"You only do things you won't fail at," Nickerson replied.

"Well yes, don't we all? If you were bad at your job wouldn't you not be doing it?" Fred asked.

Nickerson's face cringed at the question, but he didn't answer. "The thought of you failing at something you think you're good at is scary to you. Maybe you should try to do something you don't think you're good at. Experiment a bit." Nickerson was getting jittery. "If you are awful at basketball then challenge someone at a quick game. If you lose you'll know what it feels like to fail. Trust me," Nickerson said a bit hesitantly. "I've failed at things myself." Nickerson tensed up.

"Are you okay?" Fred asked. Nickerson was usually very calm. He didn't seem himself.

"Yes," Nickerson answered. "Like I was saying, a

fear is simply an irrational belief. Failing is normal. Never failing isn't. When we all realize that sometimes we can't always do things correctly, we'll be better off. Do you understand?"

Fred nodded. "So me worrying about doing badly at things is irrational?"

"Yes. Let me give you a better example, it would be normal to be afraid of a snake that you know is poisonous, but it's a phobia when you become afraid of all snakes." Nickerson's face tensed up again as he paused. "It would be normal to be afraid of a loaded gun aimed at you. But what would be considered a phobia is if you're afraid of all unloaded guns, too. It's certainly normal for you to be afraid of failing some things, but if you're afraid of failing everything there's a problem. If you live a life without failure then you may as well not be living a life at all." Nickerson's face dropped. "I know that if I worried about everything I've failed at, I'd be in trouble."

Fred didn't understand why Nickerson was acting so strange. "So you want me to see if I care when I fail at something I've never tried?" Fred asked.

"It's a start. Basketball would be a start," Nickerson answered.

"But what if I don't fail?"

"Then experiment with other things." Nickerson said without a sign of emotion. "Try something harder."

Chapter 2

Agent Hank Garrison walked through the door of an old rented out house. "How many people were found?" he asked as he looked up and down the rustic-looking interior.

"Three dead bodies," a young-looking, dirty blonde detective answered.

"Massacred or simplistic?" Garrison asked as rubbed his goateed chin.

"I'm not sure myself. I got here just a few minutes before you. I have yet to see the bodies. The crime scenes are pretty bombarded with our men. They're all checking to see if they can find anything."

Garrison smiled. "Well, Billy, it seems pointless to even search for stuff like that nowadays. People seem to hide their tracks very well. You just never know anymore. Fingerprints are worthless. Everything is contaminated. Always is."

Billy nodded. "I agree with you. But that's just the way it goes."

"Oh I know. Trust me, I do. I'm not saying not to

do it. It's what has to be done. All I'm saying is it's very doubtful they'll find anything. If you're already bringing in the FBI you know right away that this guy knows what he's doing. I've seen it hundreds of times before," Garrison said.

Billy nodded. "So there are three victims and three separate crime scenes within the house."

"Did anyone check up on who owns this place?" Garrison asked.

"All I know so far is it was rented out. Other than that I'm sure some guys are on it."

"Rented out to a killer. It's so strange how the world works. You never know who is the victim and who is the victor. You can never let your guard down," Garrison said.

Billy didn't understand what he was getting at. "Yeah."

Billy started walking over to a group of officers standing inside and outside of a small room just a few yards away. "I assume we may as well start."

Garrison was right behind him. "And no better place than the scene of the crime."

They both stopped just outside of the room and peered in.

It was a bathroom. Its once white tiles were now tainted with red blood. The mirror above the sink was shattered and glass had fallen everywhere. What was left of the mirror was splattered with blood and brains.

"Excuse me, gentlemen," Garrison said as he pushed his way through. "FBI here to take a look at the victim."

Garrison and Billy stopped in front of a thirty-something, brown-haired man who was lying in his own blood on the bathroom floor. His face was stuck with a frightened expression.

"What do we know about this guy?" Garrison asked a man slouched over the body.

"Well, Agent Garrison, nothing seems strange at all. No gory serial murderer. It's simple. The lethal wound was a bullet to the back of the head. The victim is thirty-two-year-old Michael Hartnett, from Dartmouth," the man answered.

Garrison looked closer at the bullet wound. "That's all we have on him? A guy shot in the back of the head? Why was he here? Any clues? Do any of you know what you're doing? You should know more than you do. This is ridiculous!" Garrison was angered.

The man was shocked at Garrison's outburst. "We also found that the doorknob was backwards." He pointed to the door. "The victim was locked inside."

"Now that's something big," Billy said.

"Whoever did this trapped his victims from escaping. They had no way out," Garrison replied.

The man stood up and pointed to the sink. "And when we arrived the faucet was running. So we were thinking whoever did this may have washed his hands of blood afterward, but left the water on so that they wouldn't have to turn it back off and risk leaving fingerprints."

"If that's the case, Matt, then he didn't wear gloves to protect his fingerprints from getting there in the first place," Billy replied.

Matt shrugged. "That may or may not be the case. Right now I figure the victim was standing at the sink when the gunshot went off." He pointed to the shattered mirror. "That's why the mirror is broken. The bullet traveled through the back of the victim's skull, out the front, and into the mirror."

"So that would imply that the murderer was right behind him when he pulled the trigger. It must not have been unexpected then. He would have seen the man behind him in the mirror. Plus, the door was locked, so in order for the assailant to get in, the door would have to have been opened from the outside. The victim would have been aware and moved. Why would he still stand next to the sink, facing the mirror, and not fend for himself?" Garrison asked.

"So you think the body was moved here to look like he was near the sink?" the detective asked.

"No," Garrison answered. "I'm just wondering why the victim would just stand in front of a mirror while someone pulls a gun on him. If the assailant were outside the door, as soon as it opened the victim would have turned to see who it was. So if the gun had been fired then, the bullet would have hit the victim's front first and would have come out through the back."

Billy and the other detective nodded.

"So I'm saying that the whole crime scene is odd. Something's fishy. It's almost like the assailant was already in the room with the victim," Garrison said.

"Good observation," Billy chimed. "So he must have known the guy."

"I would assume so. You don't just calmly stand near a sink waiting to be killed. Most people fight back. But he couldn't have fought back if the wound indicates the bullet entered from the back of his head," Garrison replied. "It seems as if he not only knew the guy, but he trusted him as well."

"What do you figure happened?" Billy asked.

"That's what we're here to find out." Garrison was calmer.

Another detective rushed into the bathroom out of breath. "Agent Garrison, finally you're here. We just found a video tape near one of the other victims." The man showed Garrison the VHS tape.

"Well, that seems rather important. You *just* found it?" Garrison asked.

"Yes. We haven't looked at it yet. We're trying to get a VCR set up. I just thought you'd like to know. It may be a sick sign left from the person who did this," the detective replied.

"Thank you," Garrison said as he took the video. He turned to the detective in the bathroom and then looked at the sink. "Although the running water doesn't seem like much now..." Garrison glanced around the room. "I've come to realize that when you're dealing with psychotic people you have to analyze everything. It may have more meaning than we think."

"Hank," Billy began, "we have a video tape that may hold some important things on it. Why would a running faucet be more important than that?"

Garrison looked to be deep in thought. "I have a feeling the running water could have more meaning than this tape. Or at least they go hand-in-hand." He continued to look around and stopped at the windowsill. "Who leaves a single flower in a bathroom?" he asked.

Everyone turned to the rose in a vase on the windowsill.

"This guy is telling us something. He is leaving us subtle clues," Garrison said.

"Hank, it's a running faucet and a rose. Nothing

more than that. It seems like you're trying to find something in nothing," Billy said.

"You'd be surprised, Billy. You may very well be correct, but you may also be very surprised." Garrison took a deep breath and turned to everyone in the room. "We're here to think like murderers, not like police. When we think like police we get ourselves burned. Trust me on that one. Everything in this room is a clue. Everything."

Chapter 3

"So I've been thinking about ideas for Spring Break," Travis, a well-dressed blonde started, "and I've narrowed it down to Cancun, Miami Beach, or just a fun road trip. You guys in?"

"Narrowed it down? What did you start with? You haven't mentioned any of this to us before," Perry, a chubby, baby-faced red-head answered.

"I know," Travis replied. "But I got to thinking last night. This is our last year in college and what have we ever done on Spring Break? No need to respond…I'll answer for you. Absolutely nothing. Zilch. Nada. Zippo. Each year we say we're going to do something and we end up going back home dreaming of what we could have done. Well no longer. This Spring Break we're going to party or die trying."

"Cancun isn't really up my alley financially, Travis. And Miami Beach? I mean, it's a neat idea, but it's just going to fall through. The reason we never end up doing anything is because by the times the plans happen, it's too late. We have one week left before

Spring Break. Anything that requires a plane ticket we can kiss goodbye. The prices will be so steep by now," Kenny, a curly-haired guy answered.

"Say no more, fellas. Say no more. We settled it then. We can take my father's RV and go on a road trip like no other. Meet girls along the way. Party here and there. Dabble in a few activities," Travis said.

Perry smiled revealing giant dimples on his pudgy cheeks. "I'm in. It beats nothing." He turned to Kenny. "What do you say, Kenny? A week of college-aged debauchery."

"Debauchery, huh? Sounds like someone's been studying for their GREs," Kenny replied.

"I wish some of the words on the verbal section were that simple. The practice test I've taken had some words I couldn't even pronounce, let alone understand," Perry answered.

"Yeah. Yeah. Yeah. Some hot shot is going to go to Grad school and become a big name doctor..." Travis started.

Perry cleared his throat. "Psychologist."

Travis smiled. "Whatever. Who cares? Worry about that when the time comes. Right now we're talking about Spring Break. This is life or death. Do or die. This is what college is all about. And you know what?" Travis asked.

"Let me guess. It's the only thing we've been missing?" Kenny replied.

"Yes. It's the only thing we haven't done. The cream of the crop. The crème de la crème. So stop talking about Perry's GREs and worry about yourself. Are you in?" Travis asked.

"Well, if it's do or die I suppose it would be a

wise decision to say that I am in," Kenny answered.

"Just saying that you are is not enough, my dear friend. You have to mean it," Travis replied.

"So your father has an RV and we're going to cruise the U.S.?" Kenny asked.

"Cruise it like there's no tomorrow," Travis answered.

"And what exactly are we going to do? Sex, drugs, and rock and roll?" Kenny questioned with a laugh.

"You never know," Travis shot back. "Are you in or are you out?"

Kenny bit his lip as if in thought. "What about Krista?"

"What about Krista!? You've been dating her for what...a total of two weeks? Kenny, Kenny, Kenny. This is a guy trip. Leave the lady at home. You'll find better," Travis answered.

"First off, it's been more like three months. And have you seen her, she's drop dead gorgeous. The odds that I could find better than her are slim to none," Kenny replied.

"We could have her come too, Travis," Perry said.

"No way! Where's the fun in that? If she comes she'll invite that prissy ass, big-mouthed friend of hers to come along. I will not have that shit in my RV."

"Your *dad's* RV, Travis. Remember that," Kenny said in a harsh tone.

Travis was angered. "Ah what the hell? You know what, who the hell gives a shit? Bring Krista, bring Krista's ugly friend. Might as well invite our whole psychology class while we're at it."

"Travis, you're blowing this whole thing out of

proportion. All I asked was what about Krista? Maybe she'll want me to go alone. It's only a week. Forget I even mentioned the whole damn thing. What are we going to do on this trip? What are your extended plans?" Kenny asked.

"I don't know. Wild shit. White water rafting, bungee jumping, sky diving. Wherever the road may take us."

"Sounds like the road may take us six feet under. Aren't those things a bit dangerous?" Perry asked. "I'd rather not risk my life for a week of fun."

"I just threw out some ideas. I don't know what we'll do. The point is that we'll have fun together. What are you afraid of anyway?" Travis asked.

Perry turned red. "Oh nothing. I was just wondering."

"Speaking of white water rafting, Travis, I haven't seen you go anywhere near water since I've known you. Why would you want to raft?" Kenny asked.

"Yeah, why?" Perry questioned.

Travis grew tense. "What do you mean you haven't seen me go near the water? What are you getting at? Are you trying to psychoanalyze me? Wouldn't that be better for Perry to do?"

"All I'm saying is I always found it odd why you never go near the water. Like even last summer, when we went to the beach, you never went into the water," Kenny replied.

"So what? I don't like the beach water. I'm sorry that I prefer to stay on the shore while you and Perry frolic in the ocean where hundreds of people shit and piss daily."

"No need to get rude. I was just wondering why you

never did. Thought this was as good a time as any. If you are afraid of the water you can say it. We won't judge you. It's not like I haven't told you a thousand times how I'm claustrophobic," Kenny said.

"How the hell did we even wind up on this topic?" Travis asked. "Let's just drop this whole damn thing. If I want to study for psychology I'll know who to help me. All I wanted was for my buddies to tell me they wanted to join me on a great Spring Break and now you both think I'm waterphobic."

"Hydrophobic," Perry corrected.

"Whatever," Travis muttered.

Chapter 4

"Hank, the T.V. is all set up downstairs for whenever you want to watch that video," Billy said as he approached Garrison who was surveying the second crime scene.

"Okay," he handed the tape to Billy. "You can get a head start on watching it. See if it's worthwhile."

"You sure?" Billy asked.

"Yes. It may be nothing anyhow," Garrison replied.

"Hank, I doubt this is nothing."

"It could be a home video left by whoever owns this house," Garrison replied.

"Okay, I'll give you that. But even if it was nothing, I just learned that even nothing is something to you," Billy responded.

"Then go find me that something," Garrison answered.

"I'll try." Billy walked away with the tape.

"So, Detective Tate, what did you say about this victim again?" Garrison asked a man hovered over a female victim's dead body.

She lay in bed with her head still atop a pillow. She looked cozy and peaceful, but the blood that stained the white sheets and pillowcase suggested otherwise.

"Gunshot wound to the back of the head. We'll have to see what more we get from Forensics and what not. My guess is she was sleeping when it happened. Just twenty-six years old," Tate answered.

Garrison turned to look at the doorknob. It was reversed, too.

"He trapped her, too. That sick bastard didn't give anyone a chance," Garrison said.

Tate looked at the door. "Yeah. That's how the minds of killers work. He had to trap two of them because they were all in different areas of the house. It would have been impossible to have killed one without having the others try to flee."

Garrison's eyebrows lowered. "It seems as if we may have more than one killer on our hands. Each victim could have been shot at the same time. Two, even three, murderers may have been present."

"I doubt that they happened all at once," Tate replied. "My guess would be that they all occurred at different times. This body looks much more fresh than the other two."

Garrison looked closely at the dead body. "So you think she was sleeping, huh?"

"That would be my guess. The way the victim's laying seems to suggest that." He pointed to the body. "She's on her side, her hands are tucked under the pillow, and her knees are bent inward, towards her chest."

"It almost looks fake though," Garrison replied.

"How so?"

"She just doesn't look comfortable. We try to get comfortable when we're sleeping," Garrison answered. "And it wouldn't make sense to have her back facing the door."

"Why do you say that?" Tate asked.

"Well right now it would seem like she was locked in here," Garrison replied. "Wouldn't you face the locked door if you were in here, just in case someone comes in? Wouldn't you want to be ready for them?"

"That's true. So you think she wasn't sleeping then?" Tate asked.

"I'm not entirely sure. But it just doesn't seem like someone could fall asleep while being locked in a bedroom," Garrison responded.

"Maybe she didn't know she was locked inside."

"Maybe." Garrison pointed to the victim. "But look at her. What would you say the temperature has been outside recently?"

"I'm not sure," Tate answered. "Cold. Probably in the low thirties."

Garrison nodded. "That seems about right. So how come she doesn't have a blanket on?"

Tate was puzzled. It was true. The cold temperature would call for a blanket, but the victim was without one.

"Do you think she was moved into this position after she was killed?" Tate asked. "Do you think she was killed somewhere else in this room and then just put in the bed to look like she was sleeping?"

Garrison shook his head. "No. If that were the case there would be blood all over this room from moving her body. It's spotless." He looked around. "There's not a drop anywhere other than the bed. She was certainly killed while lying here. There's not a doubt in my mind about that."

Tate was confused. "So you're saying she wasn't moved, but at the same time you're saying that it's odd she's laying like she is. What exactly are you suggesting then?"

"I'm suggesting that she wasn't put into this position *after* she was killed. I'm suggesting she was *forced* into this position *before* she was killed," Garrison answered.

Tate was in awe of Garrison's assumption. "Why?" he asked.

"That's what we're here to figure out." Garrison saw the look in Tate's eyes and changed the subject. "So one guy is shot while in the bathroom. Another is shot while asleep. I can't wait to see what's next."

"Oh trust me, you'll wish you did wait," Tate said.

Garrison shook his head. "Where was the video tape found?"

"Under the bed."

"Anything else found in the room that seemed important?" Garrison asked.

"Nope. Nothing was in this room when we came in. Well, nothing besides the tape we gave you, the body, and the furniture. We checked the closet and all the drawers. Nothing anywhere else," Tate replied.

Garrison slowly scanned the room. He smiled as his eyes focused in on a rose in the trash barrel. "I wouldn't call that rose nothing."

"What do you mean?" Tate asked as he turned to the flower Garrison was looking at.

"That's the second rose he's left," Garrison said. "There was one in the bathroom with the other victim."

Tate's eyes got big. "Do you really think that means something? Because there was a rose near the third victim, too."

"Well, if that's the case, of course it's something. That's the killer's mark. He wants us to give him a name. How poetic it is," Garrison said.

"This is some sick ass poetry," Tate replied.

Chapter 5

"So tell me, Troy," Nickerson began, "how have you felt since our last meeting?"

Troy looked completely drained. He seemed tired and almost helpless. His bright blue eyes looked like they were screaming for help.

"The same, Dr. Nickerson. I feel just as bad as I did last week, if not worse."

Nickerson took off his glasses. "How do you feel?"

"Worthless, I guess that would be a good word to describe it," Troy answered.

"Did you do what I suggested last week? Did you try to do something that was meaningful to you?"

"Yes I tried. I'm not sure if I succeeded though. I just feel so useless, so empty inside. I can't sleep. I hardly eat. I think I've slept a total of three hours the last two nights. I probably ate no more than twice in that same span. My days just seem worthless. I don't mean to sound like a broken record, but I wake up everyday feeling just as bad about myself as I did the night before," Troy replied.

"It's tough. I understand that. It happens to all of us. We all get depressed sometimes," Nickerson said.

"You don't ever seem depressed."

Nickerson looked down at his desk for a second then looked back at Troy. "We have ways to cover it up. We all are depressed deep inside, but some of us can manage it better than others."

"So you get depressed?" Troy asked.

Nickerson nodded. "Of course, Troy. We all do. Depression stems from so many things in our lives that it would be impossible for anyone to escape it. It comes from mistakes and regrets. The list goes on and on. So of course I get depressed. It's only normal. We all do things we regret; stuff we wished we hadn't. Stuff that saddens us. I'm sure there isn't one person in this world that hasn't been sad at one point or another in their life. You won't find a single person who has never been depressed. And if someone tells you otherwise then I'm sure their lying." Nickerson bowed his head and looked at his desk before looking at Troy again. "Sometimes we may even get sad for no reason. But you cannot give in. When you feel really bad, when you're at your lowest of lows, what do you do?"

"I read my history books. It seems like they are the only solace I have," Troy answered.

"Okay, that's good. Do they help you at all?" Nickerson asked.

"I suppose they do. Sometimes I get lost in it all. But in the end I feel just as bad. It seems like everyone in the books had a meaningful life. Their lives meant something. Mine doesn't feel the same way. People will always remember Lincoln and Kennedy. Those people stay etched in our minds forever. But not me. I'm worthless compared to them."

"You cannot think like that, Troy. You're a bright

young man. You told me you're the tops in your class. You're good-looking, smart, and a genuine guy. It seems to me you have more than those dead people..." Nickerson paused and started again, "than those famous people you read about in your history books."

"It's just upsetting, I guess," Troy replied.

"What is?"

"How everyone around me always seems so happy," Troy answered. "My roommate gets all 'A's and I never see him down in the dumps. My classmates always come in with giant smiles on their faces. My parents are always happy-go-lucky. I feel left out. The only thing I really want out of life is a sense of meaning. Basically all I'm asking for is happiness." Troy pulled up his sleeves.

Nickerson stared at the cut marks on Troy's forearms.

"Troy, you don't ever feel bad enough that you think of hurting yourself, do you?"

Troy looked stunned. He quickly pulled his sleeves back down. "No, Dr. Nickerson. What do you mean? I've never tried to kill myself, if that's what you're implying. I may be depressed, but I am certainly not suicidal."

Nickerson just nodded. The image of the cuts was still vivid in his mind.

"If you're asking me that because of the marks on my arm, I can assure you they aren't from me cutting myself."

"I'm not implying anything, Troy. It's just a question. From what I've heard from you last week I wouldn't even get the inclination that you're capable of hurting yourself. You're too smart for that. You have too much to lose."

25

Troy was suddenly irritable. "I know what you're doing, Dr. Nickerson. You're using reverse psychology on me. I'm not stupid. My roommate studies psychology. He tells me how well people like you can mind control their patients and get what they want out of them."

"Troy, calm down. I am not trying to mind control you. This is my job. I promise that I believe you. You say you don't hurt yourself and I believe that you don't. This thing we have here, these sessions, are all based upon trust. Without trust we have nothing. Isn't that right?" Nickerson asked.

"Yes."

"Then I trust you and you trust me. Let's leave it at that," Nickerson replied.

"Okay. I'm sorry I overreacted," Troy said.

"It's okay. So let's move on to something that is easier for you to talk about. Is that alright with you?"

"Yes."

"Good, because I'm here to help you achieve a sense of happiness. You're right, Troy, no one wants to get a sense that their life is meaningless." Nickerson stopped and rubbed his forehead. "I know that yours is not. I trust that deep down inside you know yours is not meaningless, too. I could easily write you up a prescription for depression pills, but I believe you can fix these false beliefs about your life without the help of a pill. I'm a firm believer in that. Underneath all this emptiness you feel is the real Troy. And in time I know he'll shine through. It just takes time. So let's find out who he is."

Troy was much more relaxed. He knew that Nickerson made a lot of sense and he did trust him.

If not him than whom else?

Chapter 6

"Krista, are you hanging out with Kenny tonight?" Sara, a big-mouthed girl asked as she got into her car.

Krista got into the passenger seat and shut the door. "I'm not sure. He hasn't called yet, but I think we probably will. Why?"

The car started up. "Just wondering."

"No. I don't buy it, Sara. You never are just wondering for the sake of wondering. What's the deal?"

"Nothing really. I just thought you and I could go to the mall and buy some swimsuits," Sara replied as she pulled onto the street.

"Swimsuits? It's still a little cold to be talking about swimsuits, isn't it?" Krista asked.

Sara smiled. "Yeah, if you're going to spend your Spring Break in an Igloo. We're going to go on a cruise."

Krista looked at Sara with raised eyebrows. "A cruise? Since when?"

"Since my parents bought me two cruise tickets to Bermuda. Boys, boys, boys, Krista. Hot boys!"

"Wait. I don't think so," Krista replied.

"And why is that?" Sara asked.

"I don't have money to pay your parents for the ticket and I am probably going to spend some time with Kenny over break."

"My parents are giving the ticket to you for free, Krista. And a week away from Kenny wouldn't be that bad," Sara answered.

"I can't just have your parents give me a free ticket. They're expensive."

"Trust me, Krista, my parents gamble away more money than the ticket costs. And you've been like a daughter to them the past few years anyhow. So what do you say? Are you coming?" Sara asked.

Krista closed her eyes for a moment and then opened them back up. "I'll have to ask Kenny."

"Tell me you're joking. Tell me, Krista, right now, that you were just kidding. You have to ask Kenny if you can go on a cruise? You've got to be shitting me. How whipped are you?" Sara asked.

"I'm not whipped," Krista quickly responded.

Sara started to laugh. "Yeah right. You do everything he tells you to do. You're so whipped I'm surprised I don't see cuts from all the lashes you've gotten."

"Sara, I am not whipped. That's all there is to it. Think what you will. I know what I know," Krista replied.

Sara took her eyes off the road and looked at Krista. She gave her a big grin. "Suit yourself," she said as she turned back to the road. "Ahhh!" Sara screamed as she turned the wheel quickly and wildly swerved to the side of the road in an effort to avoid something. "Oh shit!" she exclaimed grabbing her chest.

Krista took a deep breath and looked at the road to see what Sara was trying to steer clear of. "What the hell just happened? You almost got us killed."

"Did you just see that? Like a cat or something ran in the middle of the road." Sara shivered. "Ugh. I would have been mortified if I had run it over." She closed her eyes and shivered again. It was as if a chill ran down her spine.

"I didn't see anything," Krista answered still looking out the window.

"Yeah, well, I did. I hate the thought of such things. Funny story, one time I saw a leaf flutter in the middle of the road and I thought it was a frog or something because it looked like it was jumping along. I nearly killed myself trying to avoid the leaf because I didn't want to see it splattered on the road. Ugh."

"Were you stoned?" Krista asked.

Sara pushed Krista's arm. "No. Of course not. It was late. Things look different at night. You never know what you're looking at. I don't know what it is, stuff like that just creeps me out. Like I could never watch those operating shows." She shivered again. "Blood just really freaks me out."

"I guess we're all afraid of something," Krista replied.

"Okay then, since we're on the topic, what are you afraid of?"

"Put it this way, Sara, I have yet to look out a window in a building any taller than thirty feet," Krista said.

"Hmmm, you better close your eyes then," Sara replied.

Krista was confused. "Why?"

"Because I'm taking you over a bridge in about five minutes."

Chapter 7

Garrison nearly gagged when he entered the last room to house a victim. It was a kitchen. Inside was a girl, face first in her own vomit, at the table. The smell was horrific. It was enough to turn one's stomach. Garrison coughed into his shoulder in an effort to keep out the aroma.

The table was full of food. It looked like a five course meal. Salad, milk, chicken fingers, hamburgers, fries, a half eaten chocolate cake. Nothing looked edible any longer. Almost everything was sprayed with blood, brains, or vomit.

Garrison walked closer to the body, covering his nose and mouth with his tie. He stared at the gunshot wound in the back of the victim's head.

"So another bullet to the head. Nothing more," he said.

"Yes. I guess this guy is simple," Tate responded.

"I can assure you, Detective Tate, that the complexities come within his simple nature. There's something more here we haven't figured out. Three bullet wounds to three victims' heads.

Three roses." Garrison glanced at the rose set in a vase at the table.

"The victim was thirty-four-year-old Gloria Montgomery. She was from Somerset," Tate said. "She must have been enjoying a meal when she was shot."

Garrison didn't agree. "Yeah, in about the same way that the victim in the bedroom was enjoying a goodnight's sleep. How could three people have been killed without the others knowing? How could you not hear the others scream? Something just doesn't make sense. I know the other two were locked in rooms, but it still doesn't add up. This girl was just eating when she was killed? She was just sitting down at the table and eating? She didn't bother to run or try to scream for help? It just doesn't make sense."

"That's true. But the victims may not have suspected they were going to get killed. No one looked like they were trying to get away," Tate said.

"Well, aside from this one, it seems like no one could get away. The two others were trapped. But you are right. It's like they didn't expect to be killed. And that usually means they were kept calm. Like I told the other detectives, they probably knew the murderer and didn't expect him to do such a thing. But that seems almost impossible seeing that they must have been killed at different times. You said the bedroom victim's body looked noticeably fresher than the other two, so that would imply they were killed separately," Garrison said.

Tate nodded.

"So when one gunshot went off the others should have been suspicious of it and tried to get away, but they didn't."

"Maybe it had a silencer," Tate reasoned.

"Maybe, but didn't the police get a call from a neighbor who reported hearing gunshots?"

"Yes, that's correct. So that does seem odd then."

"And this doesn't even look like she was just eating in the first place. It looks like this was a buffet line more than a dinner." Garrison looked at the victim. "Look at her. The girl is thin, she couldn't have made all this for herself," Garrison said. "It's like the victims were all forced to be in these situations."

Tate nodded.

Garrison continued. "But why? Why were they all brought here? Who was in the bedroom? Where was that victim from?" Garrison questioned.

"Name was Patti Azevedo. She was from Westport," Tate answered.

"Hmmm. They all have to have something in common. Whoever did this brought them here for a reason. They were all from different towns. I doubt they were all friends who rented out this place to have fun. They were brought here for some kind of sick experiment. They were brought here to die," Garrison answered.

"Hank, you have to come see this!" Billy said loudly from down the hall.

Garrison quickly walked to the room that Billy and some other men were in.

"What is it?" Garrison asked.

"The tape, Hank. We just watched it. It's sick. This was an experiment. Whoever did this brought these people here as an experiment," Billy answered.

"What is on the tape?" Garrison asked.

Billy didn't answer; he just pushed the 'play' button on the VCR.

The screen was blank. There was no one in front of the camera. The only thing was a large white sheet of paper on an easel. A masked man came in front of the screen. He was dressed all in black. In a disguised voice he started to talk.

If you are watching this then you have somehow found your way to the crime scene. Maybe people were reported missing. Maybe a neighbor heard some shots. I hardly care about the reasons as to why you may be here, because the fact of the matter is that you are here now. I must say I deserve a round of applause from all who are viewing this. You will get a very good reading on who I am, but I doubt you will find me. If you do I will congratulate you. And I must say I will go easy. I will not fight. In fact, perhaps I want you to find me. But that's the fun of all this. It's more difficult than you think. I'm getting ahead of myself though. So let me just get to what you are all waiting for. The bodies. I must admit they were all useful guinea pigs. This was an experiment worth a thorough description. This was a lesson worth teaching.

The black-gloved hand flipped the sheet of white paper to reveal another one that was written on in giant blue letters.

EXPERIMENT ONE: Nineteen Minutes and Twenty-Nine Seconds

The voice began again.

Victim number one. The male killed in the bathroom. His task was simple. All he had to do was last twenty minutes without washing his hands. I'd have let him go free if he was able to wait a measly twenty minutes. Too bad. He seemed like a nice guy. Charismatic, kind, a real go-getter. But he was impatient. He had to learn his lesson. If you're all wondering why the faucet was left running, well let me fill you in on a little secret. It was running even before I put him in the room. He never turned it on, but he did use it. Sad to say, too. He only lasted a whole ten minutes and fourteen seconds. You can check for prints on the faucet, but I don't think you'll find any. Trust me.'

He waved his black-gloved hand at the camera then flipped the sheet over to reveal another blue lettered message.

EXPERIMENT TWO: Nineteen Hours and Thirty-Three Minutes

The voice started.

'Victim number two. The female killed in the bedroom. Her task was also simple. All I wanted to know was whether or not her dilemma, her illness some might say, was real. Perhaps it could be fixed. A gun aimed at her head would be a worthy way to fix it. Who can sleep with such a thing on their mind? Who can sleep worrying about dying? I know I wouldn't be able to. Apparently she could. But don't worry it was painless. I assure you, she didn't feel a thing. We all grow up wanting to die in our sleep anyhow. She got her wish. She only lasted five hours. Funny to think about that. Could you last only five hours with a gun aimed at you?'

The sheet of paper was flipped to another.

EXPERIMENT THREE: Thirty-Two Minutes

The voice began.

'*Victim number three. The female killed in the kitchen. I believe her task was the simplest of the three. It was also my favorite. I'll be the first to admit that some of us love food while others don't, but she happened to be way out there in the food department. She was thin; a nice athletic physique. I'd pay a pretty penny for someone like her to strip for me. Hell, I'd pay a pretty dime. Unfortunately, it was worthless. She could have lived. All she had to do was last a mere thirty-two minutes. Have a good home cooked meal, which I assure you was not poisoned, and relax. Apparently her gag reflex got the best of her. It's quite a shame. Only lasted twenty minutes. By the way, you won't find any utensils, no forks or knives, no spoons either. She had to eat with her hands. Putting her fingers in her mouth. Easy job for most. Not for her, I guess.*'

The hand flipped the page once more. A picture of a rose was sketched into the white paper.

'*I'm sure you've found my three roses among the wreckage. Let's make this number four. It's a rarity, you know. It won't happen again. Well, death may happen again, but the roses won't. You only get four. You have to figure out what that means. Are they meaningful at all? I suppose only time will tell. Only time will indicate whether you failed or did not fail. Time is what we're all looking for more of, but when we get it we don't know how to use it properly. So sometimes it's best just to wait things out. Sometimes trying to figure out what has just happened won't work. Sometimes it needs to figure out you. Until we meet again.*'

The video went black.

Chapter 8

"I'm sure you are all excited that Spring Break is coming up, but that still is a week away," Professor Randall Miles began. "I've come to a conclusion." He paused and looked at the class.

Every student was waiting for his upcoming words.

"I know that you'd like me to cancel the next two classes, but that wouldn't be right."

The class sighed.

"But, what also wouldn't be right is giving you a midterm like I had thought about doing before."

The class started getting chatty.

"I told you he wouldn't assign a test," Kenny said to Krista.

"You never know with him," she replied.

"Just you wait before you get all happy. I have a feeling he has something far worse up his sleeve," Perry added. "When something looks good, it's usually bad."

"Okay. Okay. Calm down. No need to riot here. You're all getting ahead of yourselves. Jumping to conclusions," Miles said. "I do have to keep my good name. After all, I *am* still your professor. And that means I am entitled to teach you something. So I am not giving you an exam, but in place of that exam will be an experiment."

Fred raised his hand.

"Yes," Miles said pointing to Fred.

"How much of our grade will it be worth?" Fred asked.

"It's tentative right now. Maybe twenty percent. But regardless of what it is worth, it will be reflective on your final grade average. If you choose to forgo the experiment then some people may have a possibility of failing the class. There are a few of you who are doing well and this experiment will be much easier than any test I could have given. I assure you that it's an easy 'A' if you do it. And that is a big IF. Some of you may just forget about it. Some may be too worried about Spring Break fun that they won't sign up for the experiment. But I suggest to you all that you do it," Miles replied.

Perry raised his hand.

Miles called on him.

"Where do we sign up and what are they about?" Perry asked.

"You can sign up on the bulletin board outside the Psychology offices, which most of you know are right down the hall. Some are already posted, more will be tomorrow. All of them are psychological studies. Some have to do with phobias, which will be today's topic of discussion. Any other questions?"

No one raised their hand.

Miles smiled. "Okay good. So let's continue where we left off which was on mood disorders, I believe. Now we'll discuss phobias. Before we begin, does anyone know what phobia means?"

Fred raised his hand.

"I'm sorry, but what is your name again?" Miles asked.

"Fred."

"Thank you. I'm trying to remember people's names and match them with their faces, but for the life of me I always get messed up. I'm horrible with names. I'd probably do better if everyone was just masked. That would save me from the embarrassment of making a mistake, because you all would look the same. But anyway, Fred, tell me what a phobia is?"

"Isn't it something that is irrational? An irrational fear."

"I couldn't have said it better myself, Fred," Miles responded. "A phobia is persistent fear that is excessive or unreasonable. It is irrational, like Fred said. Would anyone like to tell me what they fear?"

The class was silent.

"I know that no one likes to admit what they fear. But believe me, we all have fears. Some are trivial, others more apparent. Some are very common, like the fear of heights. As babies, we are born with the fear of both heights and detachment. So we either grow out of them or keep them. All other fears are created. Maybe we got bit by a dog when we were young, so now we fear all dogs. That would be irrational because we are fearing *all* simply because of *one*. When I was younger, I was at a water park with my older sister. I loved waterslides, they were so great, but there was a big one that was intimidating to me. But my sister told me she'd bring me with her. I trusted her. She was my big sister so, naturally, I agreed and went with her. We climbed the steps and got to the top of the slide and I sat down and she sat down behind me, her arms were wrapped around me like a seatbelt. So we're going down the slide, I'm having fun. I'm a little afraid, but not scared to death. And then at the very end, just before we hit the water, she lets go of me. I think I nearly drowned. Since that day I have been petrified of waterslides. No lie. I haven't been on one since."

A girl could be heard whispering in the back of the class.

"Excuse me, miss chatterbox back there," Miles said looking at the girl.

She pointed to herself. "Me?"

"Yes you. What's your name, miss?" Miles asked.

"Madison."

"Okay, Madison, what is it that you're afraid of?" Miles asked.

"I'm not afraid of anything."

Miles glared back at her. "I sincerely doubt that, Madison. Tell us. We'd love to hear it."

Madison didn't know what to say.

"We're waiting. I know you're not afraid to talk when I am, so feel free to answer now."

"She's afraid of the dark," a skinny girl shouted from beside Madison.

Madison turned bright red and hit her friend. "Not true."

"Well, I don't have all day, so you're going to have

to live with this class believing you are afraid of the dark," Miles said.

Madison turned to her friend. "I can't believe you said that," she whispered. "That's so not true."

Her friend smiled. "Then why do you always leave a nightlight on?"

Chapter 9

Fred went directly to his dorm room right after his Abnormal Psychology class. His roommate was lying on his back on the bed just staring at the ceiling.

"Troy, what are you doing?" Fred asked.

Troy shook his head as if to jump back into reality. "Just staring at the ceiling. Nothing more to do in this place."

"Eating would be a good idea. When was the last time you ate? I'm sorry, Troy, but recently you've been really different, and you look like you're about to die," Fred said.

Troy sat up. "Oh thanks, Fred, you know how to make the world a better place to live in. I've just felt ill lately. Not myself. You know?"

Fred sat down at his computer desk. "I hear ya. But not being yourself for a day or two may be normal, this new you has been living in this room with me for a while now. It's like you're having a bout of depression or something."

"Oh, just stop with all that psychobabble. Nobody's perfect. So what if I've been having a bad week? So what if I've been having a bad month? It's normal," Troy answered.

"Let's just forget about it. I just wanted to know why I've never seen you truly happy lately, but it's pointless, because you are right, Troy. I don't think I've ever seen anyone truly happy, and that includes myself. No one seems to feel safe in their skin." Fred looked down on the floor at all the history textbooks scattered near Troy's bed. "Did you have a midterm today or something?"

Troy looked down at the books, too. "Oh no. They're tomorrow. Well, two are tomorrow. My World War two class and the American Presidency class. Shouldn't be tough though. I was just doing some reading. I already know it all, but sometimes I find history to be fascinating."

Fred smiled. "And that would be why you're a history major. But what do you find so fascinating about history anyhow? It's all stuff that has been before, nothing that will be again."

"I don't know. It keeps me grounded. Some things you just understand and other things you just don't care for. Like you and psychology. I mean, I took intro freshman year, it was interesting, but not up my alley, I guess," Troy said.

"Yeah, it has its highs and lows. The class I'm in now is really interesting. More of the stuff I'd like to get into. Like illnesses and disorders. The other classes I've taken were more about the history of psychology and the people," Fred replied.

"The others sound more like my type," Troy laughed. "So how are you doing in that class anyhow? Let me guess, excellent?"

"So far, so good. I'm not failing. We've only had one test so far and I was one of the few who passed."

"As usual. I mean, c'mon, Fred, have you ever gotten lower than an 'A' in your entire life?" Troy asked.

"Of course I have."

"Did you nearly die from it?"

Fred nervously laughed. "No. It's not like that at all. So what, I get a little bit uptight at the possibility of doing badly. Don't we all? I mean, it's just like you said, we aren't all perfect. We all have our own insecurities."

Chapter 10

"Cheryl, I'm home," Nickerson said as he entered his house.

Cheryl walked over from the kitchen to greet him. She kissed his cheek. "How was work?"

Nickerson looked tired. "As usual, Cheryl, it's the same."

Cheryl smiled. "I'm sorry I always ask you, but one of these days I'm hoping you'll come in and actually talk to me about your work."

"You know I don't like to bring my professional life into my home life," Nickerson responded.

"I know about the whole doctor-patient privilege, Philip, but I mean telling me a little bit about what you do won't kill you," Cheryl said. "I'm not asking for classified information about your patients, just something to talk about."

"I know. I know." Nickerson walked over to a couch and sat down. "What's for dinner?"

"Meatloaf. I hope you're hungry I made a lot."

"I'm actually not so hungry right now. I feel tired. I

think I'm just going to hit the sack early tonight," Nickerson replied.

"You feeling sick?"

"Not sick, just tired," Nickerson answered.

Cheryl walked over and placed her hand on Nickerson's forehead. "You've been acting strange the past couple of days. Maybe you're coming down with something. You haven't really been yourself lately."

Nickerson shook his head. "Nah, it's nothing. I'll feel better in the morning. I'm sure a good night's sleep will fix me right up."

"Whatever you say, Philip. You're the doctor. But if I had to guess, I'd say you're having some patient troubles. And maybe if you told me a little more about them I could help you out," Cheryl replied.

Nickerson got up off the couch and looked at Cheryl. "You can drop that now. I'm not going to tell you about my patients. And, just for the record, I am not having any problems with my patients. They're all just fine." Nickerson's face suggested otherwise.

"I think you may be a little overly involved with them. I'm sure they must love all you do for them, but if this is what it does to you maybe you should stop. You said it yourself; you should separate your professional life from your regular one. As far as I'm concerned you don't do that very often. Didn't you hang out with one of your patients just the other day? Don't you think it's a little much? It's one thing for them to be setting up appointments at your office, but when they start calling the house asking for you, that becomes a bit much," Cheryl said.

Nickerson shook his head. "I help people, Cheryl, it's what I do. I cannot set hours when I'm available to help people. It would be wrong to tell my patients that I'm only available during my office hours. What if they needed my help when I'm not around to help them? God forbid, what if one of them is suicidal and they don't have me to talk to? How would that make me feel?"

"Philip, you're a good man. You're an excellent doctor. You do not have to justify those things to me. All I'm saying is that maybe you put too much pressure on yourself. Sometimes you can't change people. You should know that. Sometimes you come across people who will always be patients," Cheryl replied. "People who will never get better."

Nickerson understood.

Cheryl continued, "you can't save the world."

"I could…" Nickerson paused. "I can save some."

"This pressure will end up giving you a heart attack or something. I mean that. But I can't tell you otherwise because you will only believe what you want to believe."

"What's that supposed to mean?" Nickerson asked.

"All I'm saying is that maybe you help too much. Sometimes it seems that you become so entwined in their lives that it's almost as if you're living it with them. And there's a reason they come to you, Philip. The reason is that their lives aren't that great to be living. Why would you want to become part of that?" Cheryl asked.

Nickerson didn't respond. He had a blank stare.

"Okay. So I take it you don't think you help too much?"

Nickerson nodded. "I don't think I help enough."

Chapter 11

Travis peered outside the dorm room window. The trees rattled with the cold breeze. "We need a better climate than this to spend our Spring Break," he said.

"I know, huh? It's like we get a week off, but at the worst time possible. It's not even spring when we have our break, it's still winter," Kenny said.

"What's even worse," Travis started, "is that it's supposed to snow tomorrow."

"So? It's not like that will make much of a difference," Kenny answered. "What, are you afraid of snow now, too?"

"Go to hell!" Travis replied.

"We could always go on a ski trip," Kenny said.

"The hell with that shit, Kenny. We're going on a road trip. Hopefully we'll even get to warmer places than this," Travis said.

The dorm room door opened and Perry walked in. "Hey guys. What you talking about?"

Kenny turned to Perry. "Just the so called trip Travis has been talking about pretty much all day."

"Has it been officially decided yet?" Perry asked.

Travis smiled. "No. And the reason being that Kenny here is whipped by his girlfriend and is afraid to tell her that he's going to have to leave her for a week."

"That's not true at all. I'll tell her tomorrow. I have more important things on my mind than having to tell my girlfriend where I'll be spending Spring Break. There are midterms to study for."

"Sounds like you actually have decided that you're going then," Perry replied.

"It would be easier for me if she came with us..." Kenny started.

"We already went through this," Travis said. "Bring her if you want to. You still have to tell her though. I don't want to rush things the day of. We have one week to spend on the road. That's not that long. We have to plan out our destinations and everything so ask her soon."

"I'm surprised you didn't already tell her. I thought you would have by now, maybe after class or some time this morning. You did hang out with her, didn't you?" Perry asked.

"We didn't get into Spring Break," Kenny answered.

"You two have a weird relationship," Travis said. "What the hell do you two do when you hang out? Do you even talk? I mean, our vacation starts this Friday and you still haven't discussed Spring Break with her yet?"

Kenny huffed. "It just wasn't on my mind at the time. Simple as that."

"Why don't you just call her now?" Perry asked.

"Wow guys, what's with all this rushing of me?"

48

Kenny asked. "Do you need me to decide what I'm going to do right this moment?"

"Well let's see…today is Monday, so that means I'll give you until Wednesday to give me an answer," Travis replied.

"I have two days?" Kenny asked.

Travis smiled. "Two days."

Chapter 12

Miles sat across from his television in his living room, picked up the remote, and flipped through the channels. "Nothing."

He put the remote down, got up off the seat, and walked over to a cabinet above the television. He opened up the cabinet and looked inside. Miles grabbed a few VHS tapes and looked at their labels.

Exploring the Mind
History of the DSM
Phobias: A Documentary

"This one could be interesting," he said aloud as he bent over to put the tape into his VCR.

He pressed 'play'.

A white-haired, wrinkled old man appeared on the screen. *'Fear, it's what each and every one of us has. Some have a little. Some have a lot. But regardless of how much fear we have inside of us, we know that it serves a purpose. If we didn't have fear then we may be dangerous creatures. Without fear we'd freely jump off cliffs without harnesses. We'd cross busy streets* without looking. *Fear saves us from doing many stupid things, but can too much fear be bad? That is the question we will answer in this video. As great as fear may be in certain situations, there are others where it is useless. When we fear things that most do not, then we have what is called a phobia. Phobias are not useful. In fact, they hinder us from doing things that we otherwise may want to do. Phobias can be so powerful that as hard as we try to fight them we may always wind up losing the battle. That is unless we use the phobias to our advantage. How do we do that? It's easy; all that one must do to conquer...'*

The video went fuzzy and the screen eventually turned black.

A weird sound came from the VCR.

Miles pressed the stop button and then ejected the tape. The VHS came out, followed by a long strand of film.

"Shit!" Miles said. "Damn VCR."

He looked down at the destroyed VHS in his hand. "Damn it!"

He stood up and opened the cabinet again and grabbed three more tapes. One crashed to the floor. He looked at the two in his hand.

The Effects of Mood

History of Psychology

He shook his head and placed the tapes back into the cabinet. He glanced at the eaten VHS tape again and took a deep breath. "I could have made a better one anyway."

Miles looked at the tape that had fallen to the floor. He bent over to pick it up.

The Mind of a Psychopath

Chapter 13

Garrison walked into his bedroom and softly kissed his sleeping wife's cheek. She opened her eyes and squinted at her husband.

"It's late, honey," she said in a tired whisper.

"I know. I'm sorry I didn't come home when I said I would. There's been so much going on today. It's been a rough day. I'm working on a new case. Three were found dead in a Braintree house. Some sick psychopath."

"That's terrible," Carol replied. "I was worried about you."

"Sometimes I worry about myself," Garrison said as he sat down on the edge of the bed and stroked Carol's forehead. "How are you feeling?"

"Okay. The baby kicked today."

Garrison smiled. "Well, finally some good news." He looked down at Carol's bulging stomach and then kissed it. "Aren't you cold? Don't you want sheets?" He reached over to pull the covers over Carol but she stopped him.

"No. I'm hot right now. I seem to fluctuate. Sometimes cold, sometimes hot."

"Okay then. I'm going to go to the bathroom and then I'll be in bed." Garrison kissed Carol's forehead. "Get some rest." He kissed her stomach. "Goodnight, Anna."

Carol smiled. "We don't know if it's a girl yet, Hank."

"I know she is," Garrison replied.

"And how is that possible?"

"I'm a Federal agent, remember? It's my job."

"Oh yeah. I guess I forgot," she answered. "By the way, Keith missed you today."

Garrison smiled. "I gave him a kiss goodnight before I came in here. He was out like a light."

"He said he wished you could have watched the Red Sox game with him today."

"I told him the other day that I'd take him to a real game at Fenway this year. It's only preseason right now," Garrison replied.

"I know, but he was watching the game on T.V. and his new favorite player hit a homerun," Carol said.

Garrison lightly laughed. "And who might that be today?"

"Trot Nixon."

"What a kid. Only eight years old and he likes the game of baseball more than I ever did. Wasn't Jason Varitek his favorite player yesterday?" Garrison asked.

"Everyday is a new one."

"Let's hope that's not the case with the criminal," Garrison replied under his breath.

"What did you say?"

"It was nothing. I was just talking to myself. Get some rest, Carol." He kissed her again.

She nodded and then closed her eyes.

Garrison flushed the toilet and walked over to the bathroom mirror. He looked at his reflection and took a deep breath and then looked down at the sink before turning on the faucet. The water splashed all over as it violently hit the porcelain sink.

Garrison grabbed a bar of soap off the soap dish and began lathering his hands. He closed his eyes tightly and cringed as he brought his hands under the water to rinse them off.

The image of the victim in the bathroom invaded his thoughts. *This was what it was like,* he thought. He shook away the image.

It fought back.

The thought of the victim being shot in the head prevailed. Garrison turned off the water. He looked down at the sink as the suds quickly went down the drain. He grabbed the sides of the sink and took a deep breath, then slowly brought his head back up towards the mirror and glared back at his reflection.

The image of the glass shattering appeared in his mind. He shook away the image.

A new one invaded.

They never went away. One new one after another.

Garrison finally left the room and the visions seemed to have stopped. He walked back into his bedroom and sat on the edge of the bed. He smiled as he looked at his wife, sleeping soundly on her back.

Garrison took off his shoes and pants, and then fell back into the bed. He grabbed at the sheets and pulled them up to his chest.

Carol turned over on her side. "Goodnight, honey."

Garrison looked at her; she was his only solace from his sickening thoughts. She had her eyes closed.

She looked peaceful. Her head looked so comfortable atop the soft pillow. One hand was tucked under the pillow and the other was at her side.

Garrison went to kiss her cheek but stopped abruptly as an image invaded. He shivered at the thought.

This is how the bedroom victim looked when she died, he thought. He tried to fight back his vision, but to no avail.

In his mind the sheets were saturated with blood.

In his mind death prevailed.

Chapter 14

The clock flashed 12:00 a.m. on the side of Sara's bed.

"Another day done with," she said.

"Go to bed, Sara," Krista replied as she turned in her bed.

"I can't sleep," Sara answered.

"Why not?"

"Too excited for Spring Break," Sara replied. "Just think of all the fun we're going to have on that cruise."

"I'm sure it will be a great time, but I'm tired. Can we think about it tomorrow?" Krista asked. "You've been talking about this all day. Can you just give it a rest for eight hours? Just don't talk about it for eight hours. That's all I'm asking for."

"I'll try, Krista, but it's tough. The image of us having a blast keeps invading my thoughts."

"Can't it invade your thoughts later?" Krista asked.

Sara ignored the question. "I'm just so happy you're coming with me. To be honest, when I first asked you, I was afraid you'd say no because of Kenny.

And then you didn't really give me a definitive answer, but I finally got it out of you. Can't I just soak up the excitement? The sun, the sea, and the sand. What more could you possible ask for?" Sara asked.

"How about a little sleep?"

"You and sleep," Sara responded. "You can sleep when you're dead."

***

Fred and Troy were both at their desks reading their textbooks. Troy put a bookmark in his textbook and closed it. He turned off his desk lamp, got up off his chair, and then plopped onto his bed.

"I'm beat," Troy said.

Fred turned to his roommate. "Too much studying?"

"You could say that. Basically just too much everything. I just feel complete and utterly beat. And the sad thing is I probably won't even sleep tonight."

"I bet sleep would do you good. You always look so tired. And when you don't look tired, you look sad."

"Anything good you want to say about me, Fred?" Troy asked sarcastically.

"Sorry. I didn't mean it to be mean. I just think you should get some sleep one of these days. Perhaps a full eight hours. But as for something good being said about you, well I think you may know more about World War two than Hitler ever did," Fred answered.

"Those are very kind words indeed, my friend," Troy said. "And speaking of someone who knows so much, can I ask you why you even have to study? I mean, you never do poorly so what's the point?" Troy questioned.

"The point may be that it's why I don't do poorly. Maybe if I didn't study I wouldn't do so well," Fred responded. "And it's not like you're someone who does poorly yourself. You always tell me how great you do in your history classes. And you're president of the History Club."

"Damn, Fred, you make me sound like a total loser," Troy said. "I may do well in my history classes, but I know diddly-squat about all else. You're smarter than I am overall, buddy."

"I have to study hard to get my grades."

"And that leads me to my next question; how long have you spent studying today?" Troy asked.

"Let's put it this way, I have yet to leave this room since I got back from my Abnormal Psychology class. Barring the two times I went to the bathroom, I've pretty much locked myself in this room and studied."

"Sounds pretty bad. What could you possibly have a test on that needs that much study time?" Troy asked

Chapter 15

Garrison had a sleepless night. Way too much had invaded his thoughts during the night that it became worthless to even try to sleep. He knew it was too early to get any strong lead on what psycho may have killed the three people, but the words the masked man kept saying on the video played nonstop in his head. Garrison wasn't one for taking his precious time; he liked to get things done quickly. He had solved many murders and had found numerous serial killers before they ever could finish whatever diabolical plot they had designed. He wanted to solve this one before any more deaths would turn up in a rented-out house somewhere.

He wanted to end the experiment.

Garrison was one of the best agents around. If anyone had the ability to capture a serial killer, he would assuredly be the one. Not much got by him. He analyzed everything that was possible. Every detail. Every word. Every nook and cranny. He would do the same with the three murders. In the end, he would catch the mastermind.

But would the end come too late?

Garrison arrived at his office an hour before he had to be there, but by now everyone knew Garrison was always ahead of schedule. It's what made him do so well. Every saved hour is one less to be used on a victim.

He opened up the folder entitled the *Rose Murders*. It was the name he decided to give to the case because of the roses that were left near all the victims. He pulled out three photographs, each one a full shot of the murders.

The male in the bathroom. The female in the bedroom. And the female in the kitchen.

Three victims, he thought. *Three different rooms. But only one connection. They were picked for a reason.*

Garrison pulled out a sheet with the victims' names and laid it over one of the photographs.

Michael Hartnett, 32, of Dartmouth, Ma- gunshot wound to the back of the head. Found in the bathroom.

Patti Azevedo, 26, of Westport, Ma-gunshot wound to back of the head. Found in bedroom.

Gloria Montgomery, 34, Somerset, Ma-gunshot wound to back of the head. Found in kitchen.

Garrison picked up his desk phone and dialed a number.

A hoarse voiced man picked up after two rings.

"Hello," he said.

"Hey Victor, this is Hank. I'm sorry to call you so early, but I was just wondering if anything new turned up on the Rose Murders. Maybe something that has yet to be put in the case folders."

"Well, shit, Hank, you may have to wait for that. As far as I'm concerned, whatever you have is good. Someone would have told you otherwise if there was something new. I know how everyone thinks I get all the news first around here, but I think people respect you so much they almost forget about me. I don't even have the case with me, so I'm rather lost myself. I'm sure Forensics will call you soon. I mean, it is a bit early."

"Oh I know. Well thank you, Victor. If anything does turns up just give me a call," Garrison said.

"You know I will. I'll talk to you soon. Goodbye."

"Goodbye."

Garrison hung up the phone and turned back to the pictures.

He took out the transcript from the video and added it to the pile of papers atop his desk.

He quickly looked it over and highlighted certain parts that caught his eye.

'Victim number one. The male killed in the bathroom. His task was simple. All he had to do was last twenty minutes without washing his hands...But he was impatient. He had to learn his lesson...He only lasted a whole ten minutes and fourteen seconds...'

'Victim number two. The female killed in the bedroom. Her task was also simple...Who can sleep with such a thing on their mind? Who can sleep worrying about dying? I know I wouldn't be able to. Apparently she could... She only lasted five hours. Funny to think about that. Could you last only five hours with a gun aimed at you?'

Victim number three. The female killed in the kitchen. I believe her task was the simplest of the three. It was also my favorite. I'll be the first to admit that some of us love food while others don't, but she happened to be way out there in the food department. She was thin; a nice athletic physique...All she had to do was last a mere thirty-two minutes. Have a good home cooked meal, which I assure you was not poisoned, and relax. Apparently her gag reflex got the best of her...By the way, you won't find any utensils, no forks or knives, no spoons either. She had to eat with her hands. Putting her fingers in her mouth...'

Garrison looked over what he had highlighted and read some words aloud. "Bathroom. Washing his hands. Wait. Impatient. Learned lesson. Bedroom. Sleep. Five hours. Kitchen. Food. Thin. Gag reflex." He paused for a moment and rubbed his forehead. "You crazy son of a bitch. Why these people?"

Chapter 16

Perry, Travis, and Kenny were walking to class. There were only four days left until Spring Break. They were excited.

"Hey, I forgot to ask you two yesterday if you signed up for any of the lame experiments that Professor Miles told us about?" Travis asked.

"Not yet. When I looked at the sign up sheet they all sucked. Maybe they'll be a better one today," Kenny answered.

"Yeah, I didn't sign up for one either," Perry added.

"Then I shall erase my name from the one I signed up for yesterday and add my name to whichever one you two will be doing. We should all sign up for one together," Travis replied.

"Yeah, that could be fun," Perry said.

"Not because it's fun man, who has fun doing work? We'll do it because it's easier," Travis said.

"I don't like the whole idea of you cheating off of my work," Perry answered.

"Damn, Perry, you are so friggin' lame. It's not

even cheating, we'll all be there to do it. We'll just be helping one another out. Ain't that right, Kenny?"

"Well, he does have a point," Kenny said, looking at Perry. "I mean, it would make for the project to be done a lot quicker…"

"That's right! And the quicker we finish, the faster we pack," Travis said as he opened a classroom door.

"Hey wait. Don't you want to sign up for an experiment now? We'll get the prime spots if we do," Perry said.

"Oh yeah." Travis closed the door and followed Perry and Kenny down the hall. They all stopped in front of a bulletin board.

They looked at the board.

Fears and Phobias
Don't Panic
Scared to Death
Mood Modifiers

"They're all lame and their titles are even lamer," Travis said.

"Which one were you signed up for?" Kenny asked.

"The 'fears and phobias' one because Professor Miles said something about that shit," Travis replied.

"The 'scared to death' one sounds fun," Kenny said.

Perry looked surprised. "Yeah, if dying sounds funny."

Travis immediately crossed off his name from the *Fears and Phobias* list and wrote his under *Scared to Death.* "It's good enough for me. I'm number one on the list. It fits eight."

"You have to write what you are most afraid of underneath your name though," Perry replied pointing to the sheet.

"Yeah, Travis, put down water," Kenny said.

"I'll leave it blank for now. The mystery is worth the wait. We'll just have to write it down when we meet with whoever is running this experiment," Travis said.

"It's probably going to be Miles," Kenny answered. "When is it anyway?"

Perry looked at the bottom of the sheet. "Says tonight at seven."

"It should be quick and painless," Kenny said. "We can get it done even before class tomorrow."

"It also says we have to meet outside of the gym," Perry added. "I don't know if I can make seven."

Travis wrote a couple more names down. "I think you mean you can't make the gym. I'm writing you both in under me. I don't want to be separated and this may fill up quick."

Perry didn't like the idea.

"Put Krista and Sara's names on there, too," Kenny said.

"Ugh. If I must." He looked at the other lists. Their names appeared on *Mood Modifiers*. He scribbled them out and added them to *Scared to Death*.

Chapter 17

Billy entered Garrison's office. "I checked up on the homeowner of the house the victims were in. She's an Etta Peters. She's currently living in Washington State. We have yet to get a hold of her."

"Keep trying. Whoever rented that place from her was the one to kill these people," Garrison said as he looked back at the papers atop his desk.

"Do you think it's at all possible that the person who killed these people may actually be the homeowner herself? It's not like any of the victims were killed using brute strength," Billy said.

Garrison tightened his lips together. "Hmmm. It would be a possibility. Find out more about this Peters woman and get back to me. I think it may be something else. It would be too easy to track down someone who owned the house; it's more difficult to find someone that rented it. What I want to know is why were these people brought there to begin with. No one just shows up at a house, not with the intentions of being killed. They were all from different places. Did they all rent out the house?"

"Good questions, and when we get in touch with the woman we'll be able to answer some of them," Billy answered.

"What about the victims' families? Do we have anything useful with them? Maybe they knew about the house," Garrison said.

"Well, preliminary questioning leaves us with nothing useful, but maybe the second run through will find something," Billy replied.

"There's got to be something they got out of the families. They know those people better than we ever will," Garrison said.

Garrison's desk phone rang. He picked it up immediately.

"Agent Garrison speaking."

"Yes, Agent Garrison, this is Jim Gobal down at Forensics."

"Did you find anything useful?" Garrison asked.

"I suppose you could say that. The basics are the lethal wounds are all to the backs of the victims' heads, as you already know, I'm sure," Gobal said.

"Yes."

"But the male victim, Michael Hartnett, we found a slight trace of lorazepam in his system."

"And what the hell might that be?" Garrison asked.

"Lorazepam is a benzodiazepine, Agent Garrison. It's a prescription drug that is used for anxiety."

Garrison was very interested. "So Hartnett had an anxiety disorder?"

"Maybe." Gobal replied. "It's too early to know for sure, but if his records check out that the drug was indeed prescribed then I would say he did. But you never know nowadays. He could very well have been just popping the pills."

"Well, thank you very much, Mr. Gobal. This is certainly a big lead for us. Keep in touch if you find anything more out."

"I will, Agent Garrison."

"Goodbye."

Garrison hung up.

Billy was still in the office. "What's so big?"

"Hartnett, the victim in the bathroom, may have had an anxiety disorder," Garrison replied.

"So if that's true then the killer really was doing an experiment," Billy said.

"That's correct. If it's true, we have ourselves a big lead. We may have something in common with all of the victims. Anxiety," Garrison said.

"Call up Hartnett's family, see if they know if he ever visited a psychiatrist," Garrison said.

"I will." Billy left the room.

Garrison looked back down at the transcript.

'Victim number one. The male killed in the bathroom. His task was simple. All he had to do was last twenty minutes without washing his hands...

Chapter 18

"Did you get in touch with either of them?" Nickerson asked his slender, dark curly-haired secretary.

"Neither one picked up," she replied.

"Really? That's not like them. They always at least call if they are going to miss an appointment." Nickerson shivered.

"This means you're free until your three o'clock appointment with Fredrick Tout."

"I'm never free. My work is never done," Nickerson replied. He looked at his watch. It was only 11:30. "You can come back at around two if you'd like. I think I can manage holding down the fort for a couple of hours."

"You sure?" she asked.

"Yeah, no problem. It's not like my phone has been ringing off the hook lately. Seems like I lose more clients than I gain," Nickerson said.

"Isn't that a good thing? I mean, if they keep coming back you obviously haven't fixed them very well."

"You do have a point there," Nickerson said with a fake smile. "Well I'll lose you as well for a couple of hours. Go home and surprise your husband or something."

"I think I just may," she said as she got up off her seat.

"Good." Nickerson started to open the door to his office. "I'll see you at two."

"Okay, Dr. Nickerson. See you then. Good luck being by yourself," she said.

"Alaina, I try to help those people who feel lonely their whole lives, I think I'll manage being alone for a few hours. It will be a good way to clear my head. I've been stressing lately."

"Why?" Alaina asked.

Nickerson shook his head. "Uh, no reason in particular."

"Maybe I should stay and keep you company then," Alaina replied.

"No. I'll call my wife. She'll keep me company." Nickerson opened his office door and walked inside. "See you later, Alaina."

"Yep." Alaina smiled as Nickerson closed his office door.

Chapter 19

Krista and Sara stood in front of the bulletin board a bit shocked. "Who the hell removed my name from the one I signed up for?" Sara asked. "Now the other one is all full. I'll have to ask Professor Miles to fit me in."

Krista scanned the board. "We're both under the 'scared to death' category. It could be an omen. Maybe it will be better than the one we signed up for anyway," Krista said.

"That's not the point. We signed up for a different experiment and we didn't get what we wanted." Sara looked at the *Scared to Death* list. "It looks like your boyfriend's arrogant friend Travis wrote us in."

Krista looked at the list, too. "Why would you say that?"

"Because the first five names are in the same handwriting and the first name on the list is Travis," Sara answered.

"It may be fun," Krista said.

"We should just put their names on another list," Sara said.

"No, it will be fine. Don't worry about it."

"The 'fears and phobias' list has a lot of spaces left. We could do that one," Sara replied.

"Sara, give it up already. We're going to do the one that we're on. An experiment is an experiment regardless of which one it is. We get the same amount of credit. Let's just deal with it. At least we know the people in the group. The other one we didn't know anyone." Krista glanced at the bottom of the sheet. "Plus, we can get it finished tonight."

Sara looked at the list. No one filled out what their fears were.

Names:	Fear:
1. Travis Rogers	
2. Kenny Paulson	
3. Perry Sinclair	
4. Krista Wagner	
5. Sara Douglas	
6. Fred Tout	
7. Madison Rowe	
8. Shane Davis	

Sara looked at Krista. "We have the girl who's afraid of the dark in our group, and the brown-noser who always raises his hand."

Sara took out a pen and added some stuff to the list.

Names:	Fear:
1. Travis Rogers	Being a loser
2. Kenny Paulson	
3. Perry Sinclair	
4. Krista Wagner	Heights

5. *Sara Douglas*
6. *Fred Tout*   *Not being called on*
7. *Madison Rowe*   *The dark*
8. *Shane Davis*

Krista looked at the newly added words. "That's bad."
She took the pen and scribbled out what Sara had written.

Chapter 20

"You were right, Hank," Billy said as he entered Garrison's office.

"What did you find?" Garrison asked.

"Hartnett's wife told me that he was prescribed anti-anxiety medication to help him with his OCD. She said ever since she met him he always had a preoccupation with washing his hands. If they were dirty he would wash and rewash them numerous times."

Garrison had an inclination of the such. The masked man's words were riddle-like, but they implied Hartnett's impatience with washing his hands. "He was telling us something."

"Who?" Billy asked.

"The killer. He was telling us about the OCD Hartnett had. His experiment incorporated Hartnett's OCD," Garrison replied. He looked down at the transcript and read bits from it to Billy. "Victim number one. The male killed in the bathroom. His task was simple. All he had to do was last twenty minutes without washing his hands. I'd have let him go free if he was able to wait a measly twenty minutes. But he was impatient. He had to learn his lesson. If you're all wondering why the faucet was left running, well let me fill you in on a little secret. It was running even before I put him in the room. He never turned it on, but he did use it. He only lasted a whole ten minutes and fourteen seconds."

Billy slowly sat down in a chair in front of Garrison's desk. "He wanted to see what was more important to Hartnett. His OCD or dying."

Garrison nodded. "Yes. In the end, as much as he didn't want to die, the constant thoughts of his dirtied hands were too much for him to bear. He didn't last his required time."

Billy was shocked. "But it seemed so easy to not give into his obsessions. It was life or death."

"I know it seemed easy," Garrison started, "even the man on the video said it *seemed* easy. But in Hartnett's messed up mind, not washing his hands was just as bad as being killed."

"That seems a bit extreme," Billy responded.

"Well, I'm no psychiatrist, but sometimes people are so screwed up they need to do something to save themselves from an invasion of horrible thoughts. Even if saving the invasion of the thoughts means dying," Garrison said.

"Like suicide?"

"In a way. But these people weren't committing suicide. They were murdered. No doubt about that," Garrison replied.

"Oh, I know that, Hank," Billy responded.

"I know you do. Murdered for an experiment. They had a chance to save themselves by not giving into their anxiety, but when it was all said and done, the anxiety was even stronger than the murderer. In a way, it *was* the murderer."

"So you think the other two victims were also suffering from anxiety disorders?" Billy asked.

Garrison smiled. "I'd bet my life they were. No need for an experiment if you don't have worthy subjects to study."

Garrison looked down at the transcript again and read some more from it.

"Victim number two. The female killed in the bedroom. Her task was also simple. All I wanted to know was whether or not her dilemma, her illness some might say, was real. Who can sleep with such a thing on their mind? Who can sleep worrying about dying? I know I wouldn't be able to. Apparently she could. She only lasted five hours."

Chapter 21

"So, Fred, what are you up to tonight?" Troy asked.

"I have an experiment to do for class at around seven; I should be back early though. Why?"

"Just wondering. What's it about?"

"I signed up for something pertaining to fears. It was the smallest group available, so I figured it would be the quickest. Plus, it's the earliest of all the experiments. I can get it done and focus on other things. Less stuff to worry about," Fred replied.

"Yeah, that makes sense," Troy said.

"What about you? What are you up to?"

"Probably a little more contemplation. Maybe a little history and then, while you're out having a grand 'ol time with that psychology experiment, I'll be chatting it up at History Club," Troy answered.

"You sound so enthused," Fred joked. "And it sounds so exciting." He laughed at his own sarcasm.

Troy tried to smile, but it looked fake. "If you only knew."

"Whatever floats your boat, I guess," Fred said.

Troy's face suddenly dropped.

"What's the matter? Out of the blue you look sad as hell," Fred said.

Troy's blue eyes were almost lifeless. His body looked limp.

"What's wrong?" Fred asked again.

Troy shook his head. "Nothing. Just a lot on my mind. You know how sometimes I get like this."

"Yeah, but I think it's strange every time. You really should get it checked out. Maybe a doctor could put you on medication."

"Nah. I'll be fine," Troy responded. "I think that sometimes my mind just floods with images and stuff. Sometimes the weight of the world seems to rest upon my shoulders. I know it doesn't. I know I live for me and me alone, but it just feels like that. Out of the blue, even when things seem okay, I just fall apart. I feel burdened. But it goes away almost as quick as it comes."

"Only to come back a day or two later. I think you have a bad case of depression, Troy," Fred replied.

"Well, Dr. Tout, I don't think there's ever been a really great case of depression before," Troy said trying to cover up his sudden sadness with a joke.

"Ha. Ha. The great comedian sits before me. I'm serious, Troy."

"You think I need help?" Troy asked.

"Well, it's sad to say it, but I have a feeling the whole world needs help," Fred answered. "And I do believe you are part of the world. So yes, Troy, I do think you may need help."

"It's nice to know my best friend thinks I'm insane," Troy said as he fell back onto his bed.

"It takes one to know one."

Chapter 22

"It's obvious that the second victim," Hank looked down at a piece of paper before continuing, "Patti Azevedo, had some kind of sleeping disorder. The murderer was describing her illness."

Billy nodded his head. "Sounds like narcolepsy."

"Yes. Narcolepsy. She had bouts of sleepiness that she couldn't help. Even if a gun was aimed at her head," Garrison said.

"That would certainly make sense. I mean, you'd think people would be able to stay awake for as long as it took not to be killed. She only lasted five hours," Billy said.

Garrison's eyebrows lowered. He rubbed in between his green eyes. "They must have been the worst five hours of her life. Sometimes the subconscious is even stronger than the conscious."

"What do you mean by that?" Billy asked.

"Well, consciously Hartnett would be able to avoid washing his hands, but subconsciously he had to wash them. He *needed* to do it. It was calling for him. What made it worse was having the faucet running. Just think how difficult it is when you want to do something so badly, but can't. Now think how much worse it makes it when what you want to do is within reach, when it's right there in front of you," Garrison said.

Billy was interested. Garrison was making a lot of sense.

"Same with the second victim," he continued. "Her conscious was telling her to stay awake or she'd die, but her subconscious was telling her to sleep. She needed to sleep. She had to have her sleep. Without it she might as well have been dead. Maybe if she was shut in the bathroom she could have managed staying awake for however long she was required, but she was lying in a bed. Perhaps if you switch the external stimuli you would, in turn, switch how people react in situations. I bet if you switch the location of the first two victims they would have survived. But then the murderer wouldn't have had his fun. He wouldn't have had his experiment."

"And what about the third victim in the kitchen?" Billy asked.

Garrison looked down at the transcript and read from it.

"Victim number three. The female killed in the kitchen. I'll be the first to admit that some of us love food while others don't, but she happened to be way out there in the food department. She was thin; a nice athletic physique. All she had to do was last a mere thirty-two minutes." Garrison stopped.

"What illness do you think she had?" Billy asked.

"What does it sound like?" Garrison questioned back.

"An eating disorder?"

Garrison nodded and continued reading. "Have a

good home cooked meal, which I assure you was not poisoned, and relax. Apparently her gag reflex got the best of her. By the way, you won't find any utensils, no forks or knives, no spoons either. She had to eat with her hands. Putting her fingers in her mouth." Garrison put the transcript down and looked directly at Billy. "He said 'putting her fingers in her mouth.' The victim must have been bulimic. He implied that she forces herself to vomit."

"So we have the first victim suffering from OCD, the second from narcolepsy, and the third from bulimia," Billy stated.

"That's correct. Now the question is why were they there? Of course because they had disorders. Of course because they were part of some psychotic experiment. But why those three? How did they get picked? And were they even picked?" Garrison asked.

"Maybe the murderer is a doctor," Billy answered.

Garrison squinted his eyes, thinking about the possibility. "You may be right. Whoever prescribed Hartnett his medication may very well be the murderer. But then again, that would be too easy of a way to lead us back to him."

"Well, like the murderer said in the video, some things are 'easy.' And didn't he want to be caught?" Billy asked.

"No one wants to be caught. They may say they do, but they really don't. Everyone wants to be known, but no one wants to be caught," Garrison said. "Did anyone find a connection between the three victims? Did any of them know one another?"

"As far as I was told, no one knew anyone else. We asked the victims' families if they heard of the names and they had no recollection of them," Billy answered.

"So maybe the doctor hunch is right then. How else could someone get these three random people together? Only someone that knew all three. Find out if Hartnett's wife knew who his psychiatrist was. And then find out if the other victims were seeing psychiatrists. If they all were seeing the same one then that would tell us how they got there," Garrison said.

"Wouldn't it also tell us who killed them?"

"Part of me tells me that it would, but deep down inside I believe there may be more to this puzzle than even the greatest detective could figure out," Garrison answered.

Chapter 23

Nickerson walked out of his office to answer the ringing phone in the waiting room. Alaina hadn't returned yet.

"Dr. Nickerson's office, how may I help you?"

"Oh, hello," the voice was surprised to hear the man's voice on the other end. "This is Fredrick Tout, I was just wondering if Dr. Nickerson is free."

"Hello, Fred, this is Dr. Nickerson. My secretary left for a little while. We haven't been real busy. You still on for your appointment in a couple of hours?"

"That's why I'm calling," Fred replied. "I may not be able to make it at three. I have so much work to get done here at school that it would be impossible. But I did want to ask you a few questions, if that would be okay."

"Well, I'm free at the moment. So shoot," Nickerson replied with a shiver. "I mean... ask away."

"Okay. I've been thinking about doing that failing thing you told me about, but I'm not so sure how to go about it. I think the whole basketball thing wouldn't really solve much. I know you told me it's a start, but

I'm not worried about losing at basketball. I only panic about important things," Fred answered.

"Like I said before, I cannot advise you to intentionally fail a class just for the sake of seeing if my judgment was correct. But if it were to happen, if you did fail a test, you could just monitor how you act. It wouldn't be that bad if you gave it time. But maybe you will always do well. Maybe your attacks aren't even because of possible failure. Maybe they are from something else."

"What else could they be from? Finally when we get somewhere with why I suffer from this stuff, you tell me there may be another reason."

"Sometimes there are various reasons why people do things," Nickerson said shaking his head. "There are different reasons for why we panic, why we sleep, why we fail. I do not know yet what your reasons are. Like I told you before, everything takes time. In time everything is figured out."

"I don't want time. I want to know now. I want my life to get back on track. I can't live like this. I can't live constantly wondering why everyone else is so great when I'm not. I don't want to tremble at the thought of failing. I want to do something I would never think I'd do. I want to be the one to do something no one would ever think I'd do."

"What are you saying, Fred?" Nickerson asked.

Fred was silent on the other end.

"Fred? What are you saying?" Nickerson asked again.

"I'm saying I want to do be able to do poorly at something and be okay with it. I want to feel just the same as everyone else when they do poorly. I want to shrug it all off and move on."

"How do you suggest you do that?"

"I know of a way," Fred answered. "I've been thinking about it for awhile actually."

"What is it, Fred?"

"It's just like you said to me before."

"And what might that be?" Nickerson asked a bit worried.

"Just a simple experiment."

Chapter 24

"What's behind your back, Kenny?" Krista asked.

"A gift," Kenny responded.

"What for?"

"Just because." Kenny slowly revealed the item behind his back.

Krista looked at it and smiled. "A rose. Why would you buy me a rose?" She hugged him tightly.

Kenny kissed Krista's cheek. "Just because."

"People don't buy roses for their girlfriends just because. At least not anymore. What's the real reason?" Krista asked.

Kenny smiled. "You got me. I would have gotten you something soon anyhow. You know our three-month anniversary is coming up. But to be honest, because I know how important honesty is in order for a relationship to even get a chance to work out, I bought you this rose as an experiment slash gift."

Krista looked dumbfounded. "What?"

"Um…perhaps experiment was a bad term to use," Kenny said slowly.

Krista put a hand on her hip and gave him a dirty stare. "Yeah, as important as trust is in a relationship, so is saying the right things. Experiment doesn't seem too right. Am I a project to you? Is that what you think of me as?"

Kenny didn't understand why she was so mad. "I'm sorry, Krista. I didn't mean to say that word, I promise. It slipped out. It was a joke. You know, because of all the experiments for psychology."

Krista didn't believe him, but played along. "Okay, so go on. Why did you get me this rose?"

"Because I...." Kenny stopped as out of nowhere Travis slapped him in the back.

"What's up, kids?" Travis asked.

"Travis, we were having a conversation. Can you buzz off for now?" Kenny asked.

"Guys, c'mon now. What's the big deal? We're all friends. I wanted to say hello. Hell, you're standing outside our dorm room. You want privacy, find another place to talk," Travis said with a smile.

"Please, Travis, just go inside or bother someone else," Kenny replied.

Travis was hurt by Kenny's words. "Bother someone else? What the hell kind of friend are you? I tell you to buy her a flower and you crash land on me." He opened up the dorm room door and slammed it shut.

Kenny was turning red.

"So *he* told you to get me a flower? The biggest jerk around told you to get me a flower? Funny," Krista said.

"Can we just start over?" Kenny asked. "I mean, this started as something great and now I don't know what to call it."

Krista was still very angry. "Why are you friends with him?"

"Oh come on, Krista. You can't say that. He means no harm. Sure he's a jerk sometimes…"

"Sometimes? Try all the times. He's an arrogant prick. That's what he is," she said. "And I hope he can hear me call him that through the door."

"Forget about him. Just for now, at least. Do me that favor and forget about him. Let's talk about us."

"What about us, Kenny?" Krista asked.

"What are you doing for Spring Break?" Kenny questioned.

"I'm going…" she spun around startled before finishing as a hand grabbed her shoulder.

"Oh, sorry to have frightened you, Krista. How are you?" Perry asked.

"I'm good, how are you?"

"Same 'ol, same 'ol. Can't complain, I guess." Perry patted Kenny on the shoulder. "Are you two having an intimate conversation out here in the hall?"

"We were, until Travis barged in," Kenny replied.

Perry smiled. "So he's in there, huh?" he asked pointing to the door.

"Yes, he is," Krista answered.

"Well then, I think I'll head back out," Perry said. "Maybe get a bite to eat or something."

"Oh, so even you don't like him?" Krista asked. "An odd friendship you guys have."

Perry smiled. "I don't know him as well as Kenny does. I was dragged into that friendship because he's my roommate. Sometimes he's nice, but most of the time he's scary as hell. To be honest, I'm scared to death of him at times."

Krista smiled. "Speaking of which, we have that experiment at seven, right?"

"Yep," Perry nodded. "Meet in front of the gym."

"Well, okay then, I'll see you two there. Maybe you can work it out with Travis," Krista said as she spun around.

Kenny watched as Krista walked away and yelled out, "What are you doing for Spring Break?"

Krista turned around a few yards down the hall. "I'm afraid you'll have to wait. I'll see you at seven."

Chapter 25

Garrison stood up from behind his desk and questioned Billy as soon as he walked into the office. "What did you find?"

"Hartnett's wife said he has been going to a psychiatrist based in Boston for the past three years," Billy answered.

"What's his name?"

"Dr. Philip Nickerson. But it gets better," Billy replied.

"He's the psychiatrist of the other two victims?" Garrison asked.

"Just one other one. The victim found in the kitchen, Gloria Montgomery, she went to him sparingly."

"He doesn't seem to solve any of his patients' problems if they're dying," Garrison said. "If he were the killer he'd have few clients coming for his help."

"Either that or he'd get more," Billy said back.

"Huh?"

"The people who lost their loved ones would go to him seeking help for depression," Billy answered.

Garrison was unsure if Billy was serious or joking so he ignored the comment. "Well, either way, we have a big lead. We can call up this guy and find out who the hell he is," Garrison said.

"There's more, Hank," Billy said.

Garrison bit his lip. "What more?"

"Lots more."

"Well spill it, Billy."

"The woman who was killed in the bedroom did have narcolepsy. She was treated a few years ago for the disorder, but stopped going to the psychiatrist. Nothing worked. She tried everything and it was useless"

Garrison interrupted Billy. "And she never saw that Dr. Nickerson?"

"No. She saw some other guys. Not even based in the area. Her father was unable to answer the questions completely. He didn't know any names, but he said a few different psychiatrists from New York," Billy answered.

"Long travel for narcolepsy help," Garrison said.

Billy nodded. "Yeah. Her father said they went everywhere to stop her sleeping bouts, but nothing worked. No drugs, no doctors. Nothing. So they gave up. But she was always on edge with her illness, and her father said she joined many studies to find out more."

Garrison knew what Billy was getting at. "Or experiments."

"Yes, Hank. Or experiments," Billy responded.

"So she may have read about a study being done on narcolepsy in the paper or online," Garrison said. "All we have to do is find out who placed the ad."

"I was ahead of you on that. I'm having some guys try to find ads that fit the criteria. They're checking the newspaper archives and the Internet for anything that pertains to psychological disorder studies," Billy said. "They'll notify us if they get anything."

"Good," Garrison said. "So now we have to call up Dr. Nickerson, see what he's been up to lately."

Billy nodded and handed Garrison a phone number. It was Nickerson's.

Garrison picked up his desk phone and began dialing, then stopped. "How far is this guy's practice from here?"

"Probably about fifteen to twenty minutes," Billy answered.

"Rather than call him, let's meet him face-to-face."

Chapter 26

Sara knocked gently on Professor Miles' half shut office door.

"Come in," Miles' voice was heard from inside.

Sara gently pushed the door open. "Hello, Professor Miles."

Miles smiled from behind his desk. "Hello."

"I'm Sara Douglas. I'm in your Monday, Wednesday, Friday nine o'clock Abnormal Psychology class."

"Yes," Miles replied. "How may I assist you?"

"I was just wondering how the experiments will be graded? I forgot to ask you in class yesterday," Sara said.

"They are done on a pass-fail basis," Miles replied.

"Okay, I see. Who usually conducts the studies?"

"The studies are conducted by students and professors," Miles answered. "So they're usually simple tasks that you have to do. Some students in psychology have to do a study in order to get their degree and professors of psychology are always looking for good studies or experiments to write papers about. At this university, and I'm sure at most, a professor needs to have a published article in their field in order to obtain tenure."

"Tenure?"

"In layman's terms, basically the right to stay as a professor. It would become really difficult to fire a professor who has tenure," Miles said and then started to laugh. "Well, barring anything extreme."

"I see. Thank you for answering my question," Sara said as she backed out of the office.

"Wait," Miles said. "What study are you signed up for?"

"I was signed up for 'mood modifiers,' but someone scribbled my name out of it and added me and my friend to a different one."

"That seems hardly fair," Miles started. "I'm doing the 'mood modifiers' study, so if you and your friend would still be up for that one, it's tomorrow afternoon."

"Maybe. I'll have to talk it through with her."

"Hey, you never know, maybe the other one that you got signed up for will be better. I'm sure they're all fun. They're easy," Miles responded. "Do you know which one you're in now?"

"Yeah, the fears one," Sara replied.

"Oh, I'm conducting that one too," Miles said smiling.

"Oh, you are? So I'll see you at seven tonight then," Sara said.

Miles had a strange look on his face. "Um…no…I must have been confused." He scratched his cheek. "Did I put seven on the sheet?"

"Yes," Sara answered.

Miles thumbed through a stack of papers on his desk. "That must have been a mistake." He grabbed a sheet of paper. "No wait, I'm right, you must have been mistaken. That study isn't until Friday." He held up the paper for her to see.

Sara looked at the sheet. "No, not that one. I'm sorry, my fault. I meant the other one. The one that you can write your fears in next to your name on the sheet."

Miles smiled. "Oh....um...I'm not doing that one. But I'm sure it will be wonderful." He looked down at his desk and started putting the papers in order again. He looked jittery.

Sara noticed his jumpy hands. "Are you okay, Professor Miles?"

Miles laughed. "Oh yeah. I think I may have had a little too much coffee today."

Sara smiled. "Yeah that happens to me a lot, too. Usually when I'm studying for tests though." She stepped back. "Okay, well I will see you in class tomorrow then."

"Yes you will," Miles replied. "Have fun with the study tonight."

"I hope I do. Just got to get it in my head that it's just pass or fail."

Miles smiled. "Do or die."

Chapter 27

"May I help you?" Alaina asked as soon as Garrison and Billy approached her desk.

Garrison flashed his FBI badge. Billy did the same. "Yes, we're Agents Hank Garrison and William Boddicker of the FBI. This is Dr. Philip Nickerson's office, isn't it?" Garrison asked.

Alaina looked worried. "Yes it is. Is there a problem?"

"It's tough to say right now," Garrison said. "Is Dr. Nickerson around?"

"Yes, he's in his office right now," Alaina replied.

"He's not with a patient, is he?" Billy asked.

"No, he's not. He has an hour free until his next session," Alaina answered.

Garrison smiled at Alaina. "Well, we're here to see him. We'll be his next session."

Alaina got up off her chair and walked over to Nickerson's door. "Just a moment."

Alaina knocked on the door a few times.

"Come in," Nickerson said from behind the door.

Alaina slowly opened up the door just a little and stuck her head in. She looked at Nickerson who was at his desk reading an article. "Dr. Nickerson, two FBI men are here to see you."

Nickerson looked shocked. "What?" He quickly folded up the article and put a book on top of it. "They're here now?"

"Yes, sir. They would like to speak with you. They are waiting out here."

"What for?" Nickerson asked.

"I don't know," Alaina answered.

"Okay, well send them in." Nickerson stood up waiting for them to enter his office.

Alaina shut the door and spun around to face Garrison and Billy. "Okay, he's ready to see you two now."

They both walked over to the door. Alaina opened it up for them.

"Thank you," Garrison said.

"Hello, gentlemen," Nickerson began as they both entered. "I'm Dr. Philip Nickerson. Is everything alright?"

"That's what we're here to find out, Dr. Nickerson," Garrison said. "I'm Agent Hank Garrison of the FBI and this is my partner, Agent William Boddicker."

Nickerson motioned to a few chairs. "Have a seat, gentlemen. What brings you two here?"

Garrison and Billy both sat down. "We were just wondering if you've treated a Michael Hartnett recently," Garrison said.

Nickerson sat down in his own chair. "Well, legally I'm not at liberty to give out that information. It's against psychiatric policy."

Billy smiled as he showed his badge. "We're FBI, Dr. Nickerson, we're making it legal."

"Besides, we found out from his wife that you were his doctor anyhow," Garrison added.

Nickerson scratched the back of his head. "Well, actually he came here just last week. He was supposed to come in today, but never showed up. Never called either. Why do you ask? Is he in some kind of trouble?"

"I guess you could say that," Garrison replied. "He had OCD, correct?"

"Yes. That's what I am treating him for," Nickerson answered.

"How bad would you say his OCD was?" Garrison asked.

Nickerson's face scrunched up as if in thought. "When I first treated him it was pretty bad. He had so many compulsions, but recently he's been better. He's been on a benzodiazepine for a little while now."

"What kinds of compulsions?" Billy asked.

"What comes to mind most is his extreme preoccupation with washing his hands," Nickerson answered. "He always thinks they are dirty. He comes into the office with some wet cloths so that he can wipe off his hands every so often. But he also has to do certain things numerous times or his whole world turns upside down."

"What kinds of things?" Garrison questioned.

"He's told me that he checks to see if his car and house are locked twenty or thirty times. Sometimes more. When he walks out of my office he counts the steps it takes," Nickerson answered.

"But you say the medication helped him?" Billy asked.

"Yes. As far as he's been telling me, he's been doing better. He used to be on a stronger anti-anxiety, but he told me that he wanted to wean his way off of it. He wants to live a normal life. I completely agreed with him. I don't typically prescribe medication," Nickerson said.

"Why him then?" Billy asked.

"Well, his case was different because he truly couldn't function in the world without some sort of medication. When a disorder or an illness gets in the way of how you live your life then I believe it may be time for some type of medication to be administered."

"Did he say that the medication worked on his hand washing compulsion?" Garrison asked.

"He told me it was better, but he still was afraid of germs. I'm not sure how much it helped him stop the habit, but his life has been better recently," Nickerson said with a slight shiver. "At least according to him it has."

"And that's all you can go by. Only what he tells you?" Billy asked.

"Yes," Nickerson replied with a nod. "I mean, I don't personally hang out with Mr. Hartnett. I can only trust what he tells me to be the truth."

"Do you know if he joined any studies?" Garrison asked.

Nickerson's eyes widened. "I can't say that I do know. He hasn't told me he has. But patients always try whatever they can to see if they can fight back what's bothering them."

"Okay," Billy said.

"But what is this all about anyway? Why so many

questions about him?" Nickerson asked.

Garrison knew that the deaths hadn't reached the news yet so he couldn't just tell Nickerson of the murders. Without telling him, he was also reading him. Nickerson would give up some sort of sign if he was involved in the murders and he didn't want to make it seem like the FBI knew he might be a suspect.

"Never mind that," Garrison said.

"Dr. Nickerson," Billy started, "did you ever treat a Patti Azevedo?"

"The name doesn't sound familiar. Azevedo. Azevedo. I can't say that I have. Why do you ask?" Nickerson questioned.

Billy ignored Nickerson's question. "Is there any way you could find out just to make sure?"

"Yes. Hold on a moment." Nickerson pressed in a button on his desk phone. "Alaina."

Alaina's voice replied back over the speaker. "Yes, Dr. Nickerson."

"Can you look on the computer for a Ms. Azevedo?" Nickerson asked. He looked at the two men. "What was her first name again?"

"Patti," Billy answered.

"A Patti Azevedo," Nickerson said into the speaker.

"Yes. Just a minute." The keyboard could be heard being typed on. "No. There is no Patti Azevedo listed."

"Okay, thank you."

"You're welcome, sir."

Nickerson pressed the button again and the speaker went off. He turned back to the Garrison and Billy. "Well, that settles that."

"How about a Gloria Montgomery?" Garrison asked. "Did you ever treat her?"

"Now that name does sound familiar. It's not like there are too many Glorias around here." Nickerson closed his eyes and started to think. "I believe I did treat her."

"Do you know what you treated her for?" Garrison asked.

"I haven't seen her in awhile. It's been about four or five years since she's come in here," Nickerson responded quickly.

"Can you tell us what you treated her for?" Garrison asked again.

"Um….I'm not sure. I could ask Alaina to look it up, but I doubt her records would be in the computer. We switched over to the computer database just a couple of years ago," Nickerson answered.

"Does an eating disorder ring a bell?" Garrison questioned.

Nickerson's face lit up. "Yes it does. That certainly jogged my memory. She was suffering from bulimia nervosa, I believe. It's such a difficult disorder to treat. There isn't much that you can do, besides hope for the best. I sent her to a guy that specializes in eating disorders, I think. But all this was so long ago, I could be wrong."

"You *could* be wrong?" Garrison asked. "What kind of doctor doesn't remember these kinds of things?"

Nickerson was taken aback. "I'm sorry, Mr. Garrison, but I've treated hundreds of people in the past year alone, it would be very difficult for me to remember exactly how I handled Ms. Montgomery's case which occurred a good time ago." Nickerson sighed. "Can you tell me what this is all about? This is all a big surprise to me and I don't know what all this questioning has to do with anything."

Garrison stood up. Billy quickly followed. "We're

not at liberty to tell. It's the law," Garrison said. "We'll be out of your hair for now, Dr. Nickerson. Let you get on with your job while we get on with ours."

Nickerson got up off his seat and walked around his desk to shake the men's hands. "Well, I hope I have helped you out with whatever it is you are trying to figure out." He shook Garrison's hand and then Billy's.

Garrison's face went blank as he noticed the item that was behind Nickerson. He hadn't seen it before because Nickerson was always in front of it, blocking its view.

Nickerson saw the look in Garrison's face and nervously turned around to face what he was looking at.

A vase full of roses.

"What's the matter?" Nickerson asked as he turned back to look at Garrison.

"When did you get those roses?" Garrison asked.

"Oh, is that what you were looking at?" Nickerson asked in relief.

"Yes. When did you get them?" Garrison asked again.

"Why?" Nickerson let out a faint chuckle when he realized Garrison wasn't going to answer his question. "My wife gave them to me for Valentine's Day."

Garrison rubbed his forehead. "Wasn't Valentine's awhile ago?"

"Just a couple of weeks," Nickerson replied.

"Shouldn't they have died by now?" Garrison asked.

"No," Nickerson answered. "Well, not all of them. There used to be a dozen. Four of them I had to throw away."

"Four?" Garrison asked.

Nickerson didn't understand Garrison's preoccupation

with the roses. "Yes."

Was it Nickerson? Garrison thought. *Was the killer right in front of my eyes? Am I an experiment of his, too? Does he want to see if I will prevail?* So many unanswerable questions flooded Garrison's mind.

Garrison reached for the doorknob. *I don't have enough yet,* he thought. "We're off for now, but we may be back soon."

Garrison opened the door and walked out. Billy followed behind.

Nickerson gently pushed shut the door and took a deep breath, then exhaled loudly.

He walked over to his desk, uncovered the article, and put it inside one of his drawers.

Chapter 28

Troy was once again lying on his back on his bed, staring at the ceiling. He had so much on his mind. So many thoughts and visions. It was useless for him to shake them off; they were very persistent and would continue to invade. He closed his eyes and tried to think of a better life, a better world. He tried to envision himself as meaningful. As memorable.

He grabbed a book on the floor and flipped through the pages. Usually it calmed him down, but this time it seemed to only ignite his depressive symptoms. He stopped on a chapter dedicated to the Holocaust.

Slowly Troy glanced over the horrendous pictures of thousands of dead bodies just thrown into ditches and burned. "They had it worse than I did," he said aloud.

He turned the page to reveal even more horrors. He slowly pulled up his shirtsleeve to reveal the awful cut marks on his forearm. Some were fresher than others.

He looked down at the marks and touched one of the newer ones, and then he glanced over the page in his history book. "Maybe they weren't as bad as me." He got up off his bed and walked over to his desk. He slowly opened the top drawer and pulled out a small silver object.

The dorm room door swung open hard.

"Troy, I brought you some food, you skinny bag of bones," Fred said as he entered.

Troy jumped and threw the object back inside the drawer and quickly closed it.

Fred was suspicious of Troy's quickness in shutting the drawer.

"What are you doing? Looking at some porn magazine?" Fred asked.

Troy's face was pale. "Yeah. You caught me," he said.

Fred glanced at Troy's rolled up sleeve. "Well, that explains your naked arms. You go all out, don't you?" Fred joked.

Troy put on a fake smile and rolled down his sleeves. "So where were you?" he asked.

"I was studying in the library," Fred answered. "Then I dropped over to that Chinese restaurant just a few blocks down. Bought some gai pan chicken, pork fried rice, ching chang walla walla bing bang, and some fee fie foe fum."

Troy couldn't help but snicker at Fred's awful joke. "I'm not hungry, but I do appreciate the gesture."

"The hell with that," Fred answered. "You look like one of those pictures in your history book of the Holocaust victims." Fred didn't mean to say it and once he did he knew how bad it sounded. "Oh, that was wrong. I'm sorry."

"I think I'm going to take a nap before I have that

History Club meeting. Just leave the food on my desk, I'll eat it before I go," Troy said.

"Troy, that's a few hours from now. It will be cold by then," Fred replied.

Troy shrugged. "The colder, the better."

"Yeah for pizza maybe. Not for MSG-injected Chinese food."

Troy's face suddenly looked sad and empty. His blue eyes seemed lifeless.

Fred shook his head in bewilderment. "Troy, not again. What's the matter?"

Troy shook his head. "Oh nothing. Nothing. Really, it's nothing."

Fred placed the food down on Troy's desk. "You sure?"

"Yes," Troy replied. "Maybe I'm not going to sleep. Maybe I'll just go take a walk around campus, try to clear my mind. It must be all the exams and projects that are due this week."

Fred nodded. "Probably. Would you like me to come with you?"

"No, I'll be fine. I promise. I'll be back a little later. Will you still be here?"

"Most likely, at least until I have to meet everyone at the gym for that class study," Fred answered.

"Okay, then I'll see you later," Troy said as he walked to the door and opened it. "Don't eat my food." He walked out the door and shut it behind him.

Fred wanted to follow Troy, but decided against it. He waited a little while before walking over to Troy's desk and opening up one of the drawers. He wanted to see what he really threw back inside in such a hurry.

On top of a few papers lay a razor blade.

Fred shook his head and grabbed it. "If I leave it I'm failing at something," he said aloud. "If I leave it I'm failing at being a friend." He looked at the sharp edge of the razor blade and dropped his head in disgust.

Chapter 29

"So it seems like a pretty good lead. We find anymore on that guy and we may be able to obtain a warrant," Billy said as they walked into the office building.

"We have that he treated two of the victims. That's about it. We don't have any solid evidence," Garrison replied. "We still need to see who rented out the house and anything about possible ad spaces. We have to find out about the possible gun that was used in the shooting and try to trace that back to someone. A big help would be if Nickerson was a gun owner, but these days you can get a gun off the streets for cheap. That way they wouldn't be traceable. If anything, that would have been the smartest move. And if Nickerson is the murderer, we know he's smart. He's a damn doctor, for Christ's sake."

"But what about the roses? He seemed shocked when you saw them and asked him about them," Billy replied.

"Well, he was right though," Garrison answered.

"Valentine's Day was just a couple of weeks ago. We can't arrest anyone who has a rose in their home or in their office."

"Oh, I know that. But I just found it odd that his wife bought him flowers, isn't it the other way around?"

"Who knows?" Garrison asked. "I don't really know anymore."

"And he said four were thrown away because they had died. Didn't we find four at the crime scene?" Billy questioned.

"I was thinking the same thing when he said that, but then I remembered that the fourth rose was just a drawing. He only left three roses. But then again, maybe he threw away a fourth one just to throw us off." Garrison shook his head at his statement. "What the hell am I saying? Never mind. We cannot assume Nickerson is the killer. Not yet. He's on our radar, but there's still so much more to figure out before we can do anything. We have a possible suspect. Nothing more than that."

They both approached Garrison's office but were stopped by another agent just before they got inside.

"Hank, we got a hold of the woman who owned the house," the agent said.

"Yes. What did you find?" Garrison asked.

"She rented out the house to a man by the name of Frank Rose."

"That explains the rose leaving," Billy said.

"Did she meet him to leave the key?" Garrison asked.

"No. She lives in Washington. She told us that she trusted the guy to send her the money. She said all the other people who have rented from her sent the money within a week," the agent answered.

"So did she get the money? We could trace the letter," Garrison said.

"Not yet. She said he rented it out for just a weekend. That was five days ago. I doubt he will send the money, but she said she doesn't receive payments until about a week or two after it's been rented."

"How did he get the key then?" Garrison asked.

"She leaves it under one of those fake rock things. She told him where it was."

"Was anyone sent out to check to see if there are prints on the rock or even if the key was put back? There may be prints there," Garrison said. "I know he wouldn't leave prints, but maybe he didn't expect us to get this far."

"Yes, sir. I sent a couple of people down there to do just that," the agent said. "I also called to have the phone calls tracked down that were made to the homeowner. We may be able to find out who called her."

"How long will that take?" Billy asked.

"A while. Especially if it's a cell phone. But it will be a good lead if we do get it," the agent answered.

"Can't we find out a lot quicker where the call came from?" Billy questioned.

"Nope. I know it's odd, but it's just a hassle for the phone company to trace calls that long ago," the agent replied. "They quickly found some of her recent calls, but they said that if the phone was cellular or even a pay phone it would take time to trace. Maybe a couple of days."

"It probably was blocked, too," Garrison added.

"Exactly," the agent replied. "And to top it all off we have to do a background check on each number that we find. It's a long and tedious job."

"I see," Billy said. "Did you find anything out about possible ads?"

"I'm not sure about that. Arnie would know more than I would. I was just doing the house check."

"Okay then." Garrison turned to Billy. "Go see what Arnie can tell you about the ads and then meet me in my office. I'm going to try to figure this out some more. I have to read through that transcript again. There's something important we're missing."

"What do you mean, important? We have the guy's name," Billy replied.

Garrison smiled. "What's in a name? A rose by any other name would smell just as sweet."

Billy understood. "That may not be his name."

"I sincerely doubt it is," Garrison replied.

Chapter 30

The clock inside the dorm room flashed 5:00 p.m.

"Two hours until experiment time," Travis said. "But who the hell cares about that? I should start a countdown to vacation time."

"I'm not feeling vacation time any longer," Kenny replied.

"Are you for real? Why, because I walked up on you and Krista earlier? Give me a break, Kenny. Since when did you become the stereotypical pussy?"

Kenny was mad. "Why should I give you a break? You're the one who starts all this shit. Can you just be normal for once? God damn it. Sometimes you act so childish. Have you ever looked at yourself in the mirror? We're seniors in college. Seniors in college, Travis. And yet you still act like you're a senior in high school."

Travis was stunned by Kenny's outburst. "Okay, forget I called you a pussy. Seems like you finally grew some balls."

"See, there you go again," Kenny replied.

"Kenny, take a joke. Hey, I apologize if I ruined your chat with your girl. I mean, you could have gone somewhere more private if you were truly worried about me barging in on you. And the funny thing is, I didn't even barge in because you were outside the room. If you were inside maybe I could have understood your rage."

"How long have we been friends, Travis?" Kenny asked.

"Since like eighth grade. Why?"

"Because sometimes I wonder how we ever became friends. We're so not alike. You're a party animal, I'm not. You are loud and obnoxious at times. I'm not. Maybe back when we were younger it was fun, but come on, Travis, not any longer. Don't you think sometimes that you may be getting a little too old for all this wildness and childish behavior?"

"Oh shut the hell up, Kenny, you sound like my nagging mother. We're twenty-two years old. Of course we're not friggin' too old for this shit. This is how life is supposed to be lived at our age. If not now, when? Huh? When we're dying? When we're already dead? I don't understand you anymore. This is the time to party. This is the only time to experiment. When I'm older I won't regret one thing I've done now because I know that it would have been the only time I could have done these things. Hell man, why don't you think the same as I do?" Travis asked.

"I guess I just don't. Not anymore." Kenny walked over to the door and opened it. He walked outside without saying another word.

"I guess I'll see you at seven then!" Travis screamed so Kenny could hear. "Shit!" He sat on his bed.

The door swung open and Travis shot up from his bed. "I'm sorry, Ken…" he stopped what he was going to say as Perry walked into the room.

"Hey, Travis," Perry said. "I just saw Kenny down the hall. Want me to run and get him for you?"

"You run?" Travis asked. "That would be too much work." Travis sat back down on the bed.

Perry shook his head. He never understood why Travis was so mean to him. He tried to make conversation. "So you ready for the experiment?"

"Oh yeah, Perry," Travis replied sarcastically. "I'm friggin' dying to find out what it is."

Chapter 31

Garrison was staring at the transcript again. He was trying to analyze every word within it. There was a reason for every word. Everything had a meaning. Someone would not have gone through so much trouble without trying to make sense.

It was Garrison's job to make sense of it.

If he could.

Billy walked into the office. "They found a lot of possibilities," he said as he showed Garrison the stack of papers.

"Then we have our work cut out for us," Garrison replied.

"Do you think he'll strike again?" Billy asked.

"I'm pretty certain he will. There's nothing stopping him at the moment. The idea is to get to him before he gets to some other victims," Garrison answered.

"Well, these are all the studies they found being advertised around here," Billy said as he handed the stack to Garrison.

"Good," Garrison replied. "Now we need to consolidate them all. Only one of these ads is the one that was used."

"He may have put some other ads in to throw us off though," Billy said.

Garrison nodded. "I believe you may be right, but I'm not so sure he would have put them here to throw us off."

"What do you mean?" Billy asked.

"He may have put them here to find his next group of victims."

Billy's eyes got big.

"Are these in order from most recent to oldest?" Garrison asked as he looked at some of the pages.

"The top ten pages are from the past week. The others are from within the last month. The guys figured it would have been no earlier than a month ago when it was posted," Billy said. "But there are more. All the way from the end of last year."

"I don't think it would be back that far. The bodies were fresh. They obviously had been murdered the day we found them. The neighbor called about the gunshots so they couldn't have been there for a while. And didn't we find out that the house was rented out five days ago?" Garrison asked.

"Yes. The twenty-third."

"Okay, so if anything the studies would have to have been posted from the twenty-third, which was when the house was rented…"

"Yes," Billy agreed.

"To around the twenty-sixth. And the twenty-sixth would be far-fetched since that's when we found the bodies," Garrison said. Garrison shook his head. "No, wait. The ad must have been posted prior to the day the house was rented, because if it was rented for only a weekend it wouldn't give the murderer enough leeway between getting viable candidates for his experiments. He wouldn't have assumed he'd get three people to show up for his study. He had to know ahead of time."

"So he'd have posted the ad from around a week before the day he rented it out to possibly the last day he rented it out?" Billy asked.

"Yes. Which means from the sixteenth to the twenty-sixth. Those would be the best dates to start," Garrison said as he looked at the dates on the pages. He pulled out about four sheets of paper from the stack. All of them had been from February 16th to the 26th.

"You look at these two," Garrison said as he handed the sheets to Billy. "Get back to me if you see anything suspicious." Garrison also handed the leftover stack to Billy. "Have some guys check for anything suspicious in these. Just in case."

Billy nodded and walked out of the office.

Garrison looked down at his two sheets and looked at the headings.

ARE YOU HAPPY?

NEED HELP?

A STUDY TO GET YOUR LIFE BACK ON TRACK

MOOD MODIFIERS

DYING TO GET RID OF YOUR ILLNESS?

HELP IS JUST AROUND THE CORNER

CONQUER YOUR GREATEST FEARS

Garrison looked underneath each ad and noticed that they all had the person who was conducting the experiment. Only two caught his eye. He read them further.

CONQUER YOUR GREATEST FEARS
It's simple and easy. If you fear the
disorder you are suffering from then join the
most helpful study available. We cannot guarantee
results, but it is worth a try. Study will be held on
February 26th. Call Bridgewater University and
ask to be connected to Dr. Randall Miles
to get more information.

DYING TO GET RID OF YOUR ILLNESS?
If you are, here's a study that can help you do so.
Failure is not an option. Easy tasks to help
you solve your frustrations. Sleeping disorders,
eating disorders, and anxiety disorders most
welcome.
No need to call to set up an arrangement.
If you choose to join meet at Bridgewater
University,
outside of the main entrance on February 26th at 8 a.m.
Transportation will be provided to the study site
Thank you.
Dr. Bert Over

Garrison stared at the advertisements and circled them. They both had to do with Bridgewater University and neither gave out a direct number. They also both had the date that the bodies were found.

The second sounded more suspicious; it included everything that had to do with the murders. The provided transportation to the 'site' and even the types of disorders that were used. In a way it was almost too suspicious. And sometimes that's a dead giveaway to being a ploy.

Sometimes.

Garrison quickly scanned the second sheet of paper. No advertisements got his attention. He looked down at the first sheet and at the two names conducting the experiment. One of them was possibly the murderer. He wrote down the names atop the piece of paper.

Dr. Randall Miles

Dr. Bert Over

He quickly looked over the ads again. He stopped at *Mood Modifiers*. "Dr. Miles is part of this one, too," he said aloud. "Oh, Dr. Miles are you and Dr. Over one and the same? Are you both Frank Rose? Or is this just a ploy to lead me in the wrong direction?" Garrison circled the names and grabbed the phone on his desk.

"I'll find out."

Chapter 32

Miles turned off the light to his office and slowly shut the door. Just as it closed he heard the phone ring.

He looked at his watch. 6:04 p.m.

"Ah, it's too late. They'll leave a message," he said.

He walked over to the bulletin board and looked at the studies that were stapled to it. He tore the *Scared to Death* one down and looked at it. He smiled at what had been scribbled out under the 'fears' category. "Hhmmm." He crumbled up the sheet of paper and threw it in the garbage.

* * *

Nickerson walked out of his office and looked at Alaina. "Well it's that time of the day again," he said. "Back home we go."

Alaina smiled. "Quite a strange day, too."

"Indeed it has been. Cancelled appointments. No shows. And the FBI. Can't get much stranger than that."

120

"I hope not," Alaina replied.

"So you doing anything fun tonight?" Nickerson asked.

"Not particularly. I think Henry's inviting his friend over to join us for dinner."

"What will you be eating?" Nickerson asked.

"By the time I get there it might be just some Chinese take-out."

"That's not too bad," Nickerson said. "Good Chinese food will always make for a good night."

"I know, but it also will make me look like I don't know how to cook. What about you? You going straight home to see Cheryl?" Alaina asked.

"Not straight home, but I'll eventually end up there. Maybe I'll pick up some Chinese for her on my way home."

Alaina smiled. "What a good husband."

"I try. At least she hasn't left me. My patients may have, but she's stuck around," Nickerson said.

"Well, it's like you say in the vows, 'til death do you part.'"

* * *

Fred was in the gym shooting around a basketball. It was still more than a half hour until the study was to begin, but he felt awkward being stuck in his dorm doing nothing. He decided to listen to Dr. Nickerson's suggestion and play a sport he had no interest in.

He was alone though. So he had no chance to lose.

Perry walked into the gym and saw Fred playing around. "Hey, you're in the Abnormal Psychology class

121

with me, right?" Perry asked as Fred jumped for a lay-up.

Fred was startled. The basketball spun around the rim before falling out.

He missed.

Fred stepped on the basketball before it rolled away and looked at Perry. "Yeah. I'm Fred. What's your name?"

"Perry. You part of tonight's experiment?"

"Yeah. I signed up for it. Are you?" Fred asked.

"Yeah. I'm not normally this early, but my roommate has been a pain in the ass recently."

"Oh, I'm not usually early either. I just had nothing else to do," Fred replied.

"You play basketball?" Perry asked.

Fred smiled. "No. I've never really played before in my life. When I was younger I would just shoot around, but I was never on a team or anything like that. I'm not good at it at all."

Perry chuckled. "Neither am I. I always loved the game, but my physique wouldn't get me very far. When I was younger I wanted to be a professional basketball player, but now I've decided on becoming a psychologist."

"I'm sure it will be lucrative," Fred answered. "There are so many people that need help; you're probably going to make more money than a basketball player anyhow."

"I doubt that," Perry responded. "You want to play HORSE?"

"Is that the game that if I miss the shot you took I get an 'H' until someone spells out the word?"

"That's correct. You ever play before?"

"When I was little, maybe. Like I said, I'm not any good so I hardly ever play basketball," Fred answered.

"Would you like to play a friendly game now, while we wait?" Perry asked.

Fred looked nervous. "I'd rather not. You'd beat me anyhow."

"Oh, come on. There's nothing else you can do. You can't be that bad," Perry said.

Fred's hands were slightly trembling. A bead of sweat rolled down his forehead. *I have to fail at something. Now's as good a time as any,* he thought.

"Okay," Fred replied.

"Okay, you can shoot first. Anywhere you want, just take a shot," Perry said.

Fred stood a few feet behind the hoop and was about to take a shot.

"That may be a little close. The object is to try and get me to miss the same shot you're taking. I think I'll get that one in," Perry said.

Fred smiled. More sweat dripped down his face. He backed up to the foul line and looked at Perry.

Perry nodded. Fred bent his knees and threw the ball at the hoop. It rattled off the rim and bounced back to him.

"Not bad," Perry said. "I hate foul shots."

Perry grabbed the ball and got behind the three-point line. He threw the ball in the air and it swished into the basket. "I'm better far away."

Fred rebounded the ball and walked to where Perry was standing. He threw the ball in the air. It didn't even reach the basket.

"No worries. We all get air balls every now and again," Perry said. "So you have an 'H.'"

Perry stood a few feet to the right of the foul line and took a shot. Again it swished in.

"I'm lucky tonight," Perry said with a smile. "It's like I'm dead on. Trust me, it's not normal."

"Maybe you should rethink your future occupation," Fred said.

He was still trembling. He could feel his heart pound against his chest. He bent his knees and took the shot.

It bounced off the backboard. "You have 'H' and 'O' now," Perry said.

Perry retrieved the ball and noticed Fred's face. It was pale. Fred's body was shaking wildly and he had sweat stains under his armpits. His hair was quickly becoming wet.

"Man, are you okay?" Perry asked.

"Not really. I don't feel too well. I think I'm going to get a drink," Fred answered in a jumpy voice.

"Take your time," Perry said.

* * *

Troy got back to his dorm room and sat at his desk. He opened up the bag of Chinese food and set it to the side. He noticed a note attached to the bag.

Troy, I left early for the experiment thing. I hope you eat some of this. I'll see you later tonight when the experiment is over. We'll talk some more.

Troy opened up a history book on World War II and turned to a random page. He ripped off the note from the bag and opened up his drawer to place it inside. He was shocked to see that the razor blade was missing.

* * *

"Let's head out now," Krista said as she got up from her desk chair.

"We still have about fifteen minutes until we have to meet. The walk is like two minutes. I'm not going to be stuck waiting. We'll leave at five of," Sara responded.

"What's the big deal?" Krista asked.

"First of all, you just want to go now so that you'll beat Kenny there. I know how you are. You try to get to places first because you're afraid of how foolish you'll look if someone is there first, just staring at you as you walk. Then you get all tense and shit. I've seen it happen before," Sara said.

"That's definitely not me. You must be thinking of another girl."

"No, it's you. I know. You'll see Kenny when we get there. Most likely he'll be late anyhow. I don't know how you can even be with a guy whose friend is that big of a bastard."

"It's his friend, Sara. It's not him."

"We are who we hang out with," Sara replied.

"I think you mean we are what we eat," Krista responded.

"Same difference," Sara said. "Either way, if you want to talk to Kenny I'm sure waiting ten minutes won't kill you."

* * *

"All I'm asking is for you to be civil next to Krista and her friend. How easy is that? Such a simple task, Travis. Do it for me," Kenny said as he walked beside Travis.

"For you, Ken, I will try. I'll experiment a little.

Shit, maybe I'll even like the whole shitty ass feeling of being nice," Travis replied.

"You see, there you go again. Come on, Travis, go a night without being so childish."

"I was just joking, Kenny. Since when did you become so uptight?"

"Just be friendly tonight. I know that you despise Sara for some reason…"

Travis interrupted. "I don't despise her; I just think she's a hideous, prissy-ass princess. But I'll behave for tonight. Maybe I'll even get her to use her big mouth on me." He nudged Kenny with his elbow. "You know what I mean?"

Kenny stared at Travis without cracking a smile. "Please don't start, Travis. We're almost there; I don't want you to act like this now. I'm serious."

Travis smirked. "How serious are you?"

"Dead serious."

Chapter 33

Billy walked into Garrison's office with a blank look on his face. Garrison hung up the phone. He had tried to get in touch with Miles numerous times, but to no avail.

Garrison looked at Billy. "Anything?"

"Nothing that looked suspicious. Most of the sheets you gave me had nothing to do with stuff that pertained to the victims' disorders. Did you find anything?"

"Two ads caught my eye," Garrison answered.

Billy walked over to the desk and looked at the ads Garrison had circled.

"Did you have anyone see who ran these ads?" Billy asked.

"Yes. One was paid for with a check, by the same guy conducting the study, Randall Miles. The other was paid for by a money order under Adam Johnson," Garrison replied.

"Do we have anything on either?"

"I've been trying to get in touch with the Miles guy, but I haven't reached him yet. He wasn't in his office and I got his home number, but he isn't there either," Garrison answered.

"And what about the other guy?"

"No number, and money orders are pretty much untraceable. You don't need to use your real name," Garrison replied.

"So we could go down to Miles' house and pay him a visit," Billy said.

"We could, but what good would that do if he's not there? He could be setting up his next experiment now, for all we know," Garrison said.

"And we have no starting point to find the Johnson guy?" Billy asked.

"Not really. But he may be someone at the Bridgewater University campus. Both ads are from there. A third ad was placed by Miles as well."

"Bridgewater isn't very far. We could go now and check things out," Billy said.

"I'm not so sure on how much use that would be. I checked for an Adam Johnson at Bridgewater University. No such guy by the name. No students or professors. No one. It's a false name, so the search would be way too difficult to file down. The only good it would do is to talk to some people who may know Miles," Garrison said.

"Did Miles check out?" Billy asked.

"Yes. It's a real name. He's a psychology professor at the college," Garrison answered.

"Well, that makes sense. It was a psychology experiment and he is a psychology professor. You said you need a smart guy to pull this off. So far we have a psychiatrist and a psychology professor. Two smart professions."

"I know we do. It's not what we have that scares me. It's what we don't have," Garrison said.

"Do you have any suggestions?" Billy asked.

"A couple, actually. We can check to see if any more houses or places were rented out recently. If this guy is conducting another experiment he'll need somewhere to do it. We could also go down to Bridgewater like you suggested, but I'm not too sure that will do much help. And finally we could see if any ads that have been posted recently are as suspicious as the ones we just looked at."

"So you think he's going to strike soon then?"

"Better safe than sorry," Garrison replied.

Chapter 34

Only seven people stood outside of the gym when a large van pulled up.

It was 7:02 p.m.

Everyone looked at the masked driver as he got out and walked around to greet the people.

"Hello, all." He counted the members. "I see there are only seven of you. I thought eight people signed up."

"Maybe he dropped out because he thought he needed a Halloween costume," Travis shouted from behind Kenny. "Why the mask?"

The man looked at Travis, although you couldn't see his eyes. "Studies work better when you don't know who is conducting them. I swear to you. Well then, we better be on our way now. This shouldn't take too long. If all goes well, you'll be back here in less than two hours. Let's just hope this experiment is not a failure."

One by one the seven students got into the van. It was tight, but manageable.

The man closed the sliding door of the van and walked around to the driver's side and got in.

"Don't you think this is a bit sketchy?" Sara asked.

"I don't, but I suppose you do. You can get out now and just fail the study you have to do. Would that be a better option?" the man asked.

"Not with her grades," Travis replied.

Kenny shoved Travis.

"Okay, so we are off." The man grabbed some paper and pens from the front of the van and passed them around. "Take a sheet and write your name and your greatest fear. This study won't work unless you do that and no one did before. You can fold it up if you want. You won't need to tell everyone your fear. It will be confidential, I assure you."

Everyone took a sheet of paper and they each shared the available pens.

"I don't want any wise-asses either. If you do not put down what you really fear this whole experiment won't work and you will fail," the man said.

"How far away is this place?" Kenny asked.

"Not very far. It's a nice place, too. Right near a little lake. Secluded so that we can get the most out of our experience," the man said.

"This is really weird. Can you just tell us who you are?" Krista asked.

"Not yet, but if you do everything I say, I will show you. Only once the whole experiment is over. If you're worried about me bringing you to some sick and twisted place to kill you or something…"

Perry shivered at the thought.

"Then you should be." The man let out a wicked laugh. "No, I'm just kidding."

No one joined in on the laugh.

"Wow, I didn't think I'd have so many uptight

people in this study. There's food there if you haven't eaten dinner yet. This is a professional study. We do it and we get out. You should be honored to have me bring you somewhere other than that school. It seems like you're always stuck there. Maybe it's best you get out and do something. You'll like it. I promise. But once again, you can back out if you want. It would be a long walk, but you're all young and in shape. You'd find your way. Studies always allow you to back out if they are too much for you to take. It's not like you signed your name in blood or gave up your soul. If you want to back out just tell me and I'll stop right here. No one's got a gun to your head."

No one answered.

"Okay, well if you're all set with writing down your fears on the papers I'd appreciate it if you passed them up to me."

The folded up sheets started to flow to the front. The man grabbed them with his gloved hand and placed them in his jacket pocket. "Thank you. We will be there shortly."

Chapter 35

Garrison was looking over the transcript again. His desk was crowded with papers. Advertisements, photographs, crime scene write-ups, and everything else. It was clustered with notes and scribbles.

Swarming with clues.

Billy walked into the office. "No ads turned up that seemed relevant."

Garrison looked up from his desk. "Not one conducted by any of those three names I gave you?"

"Nope. There weren't any new Miles studies, no Over studies, no Johnson studies, and I even checked for any done by Rose. Not one," Billy replied.

Garrison huffed. "This is going to be more difficult than I suspected. It's like we're so close, but yet so far away."

"Did you try calling Miles again?" Billy asked.

"Yes. Still no answer," Garrison said.

"So we may have to wait this one out then, huh?"

Garrison was shocked at Billy's question. "No way. We cannot afford to wait this one out."

"Oh, no. Sorry, Hank. I didn't mean wait the case out. That would be preposterous. I meant wait out Miles," Billy tried to make himself sound better.

Garrison's face went back to normal. "Yes. Like I said, it would be pointless for us to go to his house. It could set us back, especially if he's not there."

"True. But we could send some men there just in case. Post them outside his house. See if they find anything suspicious," Billy said.

"We can't have a stakeout there, Billy. We have nothing on this guy yet," Garrison shot back.

"It wouldn't have to be a stakeout," Billy replied. "Just send two guys there to see if he's there. Maybe his phone is dead. We can continue with things here. See what we can figure out, but it's worth it to send some guys there for now. If he is a suspect we need to find out."

"Well, in that case, we may as well send some guys over to Nickerson's house, too," Garrison sarcastically responded. "We can't use men freely around here. They all have jobs. We can't send people off whenever we get a hunch."

"Okay," Billy said.

"There's something more important in front of us than whatever may lie in Bridgewater or in Nickerson's office. We just have to see what it is. This guy wants us to figure him out. We're his experiment." Garrison grabbed the transcript paper and read from it.

"Experiment one. Nineteen minutes and twenty-nine seconds. Experiment two. Nineteen hours and thirty-three minutes. Experiment three. Thirty-two minutes." Garrison stopped and looked at Billy. "Why such arbitrary numbers? What is his point?"

"Maybe those are the threshold numbers for the disorders. Maybe the killer knew how long they could last and he was trying to make them last a bit longer. Perhaps their longest goal was just shy of the time limit he picked and he wanted to see if they could go longer," Billy answered.

"When I first read this I also thought that. But now it doesn't seem right," Garrison said.

"Why is that?"

"Because if it was their threshold, how did he know it?" Garrison asked.

"Probably because they told him. It was an experiment," Billy replied.

"I know, but that's too strange. I doubt they would know their thresholds themselves, and unless he did a study on them before, I doubt he would know them either," Garrison said.

"Maybe he did. Maybe he knew what they could do," Billy responded.

"If that were true it would lead us back to someone that knew them. Someone that treated them," Garrison replied.

"Someone like Nickerson," Billy added.

"Or even still, someone like the men who ran those ads. Whoever they may be. Whoever it is is smart. We know that."

"And they have some sort of knowledge about psychology," Billy added.

"Yes." Garrison looked back down at the transcript. "He only lasted a whole ten minutes and fourteen seconds. She lasted only five hours. If whoever did this knew of a threshold they had before, if he knew of a peak they once reached, then they would have lasted longer than they did. The woman in the bedroom only lasted five hours. She was fourteen hours shy of the required time. It wouldn't make sense."

"Maybe the numbers are just arbitrary then. Maybe they have no meaning whatsoever, other than to throw us off," Billy said.

Garrison shook his head. "I don't buy that either. His words make sense. They all have a meaning. Those numbers mean something."

Chapter 36

The van traveled down a long dirt road with trees on each side. It finally stopped outside of a quaint, little brown house. All the lights were on inside. It seemed to smile at its visitors.

It was happy to see them.

"Okay," the masked man began as he turned off the ignition, "we're here. Now part of the study is that we have no outside interference, thus the seclusion, so if anyone happened to bring their cell phones, just leave them inside of the van. You'll be able to use them once the study has ended."

A universal sigh could be heard from inside the van.

"Seriously, guys and girls, it's not that big of a deal. You can call your parents, your significant others, even the police once the experiment has concluded. I'm sure two hours away from the cellular devices won't kill you. I bet you won't get service here anyway. So just leave them on your seats and get out of the van. Let's head inside," the man said.

Whoever had cell phones left them on the seats and

got out of the van. Once everyone was outside, the masked man locked the van doors.

"Follow me," he said. "Like I said before, there is food inside. So if anyone is hungry you can help yourselves while I set everything up."

He opened up the front door and everyone followed him inside.

The house had a large banquet-like table set up covered with food. Sandwiches, crackers, hamburgers, chicken, soda.

"This is what I'm talking about," Travis said as he looked at the assortment of food. He hit Perry's back hard. "You must like what you see."

"I will be right back, I just have to go down into the cellar and set up," the man said as he walked away from the table.

"This place is giving me the creeps. This all seems so strange. Maybe we should have backed out when we had the chance," Krista said to Kenny.

"Oh, so you're talking to me now, huh?" Kenny asked back.

"Yes I am. I'm sorry I overreacted before. Let's just put it behind us," Krista said.

"I was hoping you'd say that." Kenny kissed her cheek. He looked around the house. "It does seem a bit creepy, but what's the worst that can happen, we're seven to his one. We could take him down if we wanted," Kenny joked.

Krista smiled. "Yeah. The whole thing just seems odd. That's all."

Perry tapped Kenny on the back. "What is going on here? This is like something straight out of a horror flick."

"Guys, guys, guys. What are you all whining about? We have a table full of food. We're amongst friends. I was thinking this study would be lame, but I was definitely wrong," Travis said loudly.

Some of the other students laughed.

"Well, I'll pretty much do anything for an easy 'A,'" Sara said.

Travis laughed as he took a bite out of a sandwich. "Don't you mean an easy lay?"

"Go to hell, asshole," Sara replied.

Kenny glared back at Travis.

"Oh, I'm sorry, man," Travis said.

"Hey, Travis," Krista started, "what's your problem anyhow?"

"Not really sure, exactly," Travis said with his mouth full.

* * *

The masked man stood in the darkened, cold cellar and pulled on a string from a light bulb that hung above him. The light dimly shined.

He pulled out the folded up pieces of paper from his pocket and looked at all that had been written. "Perfect," he said as he read each fear to himself.

He glanced around the room. It was dirty and gross. Spiders and insects crawled up and down the walls and on the floor.

"This will do just fine," he said.

Slowly he walked over to the window and looked outside. The moonlight glistened on the pond.

"Wonderful."

He looked to the left of the pond and noticed a very tall tree. He smiled.

"Maybe."

Slowly he turned around and walked over to a small closet. He opened it up and looked inside. It was a tight cramped up space, full of folding chairs and blankets.

The man smiled and walked up the steps.

He walked over to the table. "Okay guys I would like you to follow me right upstairs into the waiting room."

"We have to wait? I thought we were all going to do this study together," Perry said nervously.

"Not exactly. This is designed so that you each have your chance in the spotlight. Follow me, please." The man walked up the steps and stopped outside of a bedroom. "You can all wait in here for a few minutes. Have fun."

"We will," Travis said as he ran over and plopped down on the bed.

The others walked into the room and dispersed themselves once inside.

"I will be right back," the man said as he closed the door.

"This gets weirder by the minute," Krista said. "Where the hell did he go?"

"Yeah, this is starting to freak me out," Perry said. "He said we can call it off at any time. Maybe we should just all bow out as a group."

"No, wait. Think about it. This is an experiment, right?" Kenny asked.

"I think so, but who the hell knows anymore? I'd

rather receive a failing grade than be held hostage by some psycho," Perry replied.

"But maybe this is the whole experiment," Kenny responded. "Maybe he is doing this to scare us. He may want to just see how many of us drop out before the two hours he said it was. The title of the experiment was 'scared to death.' That says it all. He wants to scare us. Let's just wait it out. Two hours, tops."

"Let's hope," Perry said.

"I don't want to fail. I'll wait this out until the world ends," Sara said.

"Not me. I'm freaked out enough as it is. Kenny, just come with me to tell that crazy man that I want to call it off," Krista said.

"Are you sure?" Kenny asked. "We'll be together. What are you afraid of?"

"I'm sure. Just come with me." Krista walked over to the door and turned the knob. Her face dropped.

Kenny noticed her frightened look. "What is it?"

She removed her hand from the knob. "It's locked."

"Well, unlock it, Sherlock," Travis said.

"I can't. It's locked from the outside. The knob is backwards."

* * *

The masked man was inside the kitchen writing on some pieces of paper. Once he was finished, he stuffed them into his jacket pocket.

He walked outside and unlocked the van's passenger door then stuck the key into the glove compartment and turned it. The compartment popped open. He reached inside and grabbed a small black box and two guns. He glanced at the back of the seats in the back of the van and picked up a small silver cell phone.

"Let the experiments begin."

Chapter 37

"We have to dissect this masked man's words one by one. Everything is a piece to the puzzle. We cannot leave even one word unturned," Garrison said as he looked down at the transcript.

"So far what do we have?" Billy asked.

"Well, we have leads on Nickerson and Miles. I suppose we could call Nickerson and see where he is now? See if he's up to anything strange. Miles has been out of reach," Garrison replied.

"Then let's call. We have to deal with what we've got. Nickerson is an intelligent man. He knew two of the victims. He had roses in his office. And fits the psychology background, he would be a possibility for having studies done," Billy said.

Garrison picked up his desk phone and pressed a button. "Hello, can you find out a Dr. Philip Nickerson's home phone number for me, please. Get back to me when you get it."

"It shouldn't take very long," the voice replied.

"Okay." Garrison hung up the phone.

Billy looked at him. "We also have Miles. Another intelligent man. Background in psychology. Bridgewater location, which is where the suspicious ads took place."

Garrison nodded. "Yes, both seem viable at this point. But both cannot be the killer. And it's quite possible neither is."

"Maybe there were two murderers," Billy said.

"I originally thought that, too." Garrison rubbed his forehead. "It doesn't seem right though. This man worked alone. He gave us as many clues as he possibly could without telling us who he is. He wants us involved. He wants us to get so close that we can taste it."

"But in the end he wants us to fail," Billy added.

"That's what I'm afraid of," Garrison replied.

Billy jumped as the desk phone rang loudly. Garrison picked it up.

"Hello," he answered.

"Yes, Dr. Nickerson's number is 555-6783," the voice said.

Garrison wrote down the number on a piece of paper. "Okay, thank you very much."

"You're welcome."

Garrison hung up the phone and turned to Billy.

"We'll try calling Nickerson now, see if he has a connection to Bridgewater University," Garrison said.

"Good idea. If he does, we have the biggest lead yet," Billy said.

Garrison shook his head. "No lead is big enough unless it leads us right to the murderer."

144

He picked up the phone and began dialing.

'Ring. Ring. Ring.'
"Hello," a woman's voice answered.

"Hello, ma'am. This is Agent Hank Garrison of the FBI. Is this the Nickerson residence?"

"Yes it is," the lady replied.

"Okay, good. Is Dr. Nickerson in? We spoke earlier today. I was just calling to ask him a couple more questions."

"What is this about? Did he do something wrong?"

"Oh, no. Nothing to be alarmed about. Is he in?" Garrison asked.

"Actually he's not. He got out of work at six o'clock and he said he had some errands to run before he got home," the lady replied.

Garrison looked at his watch.

7:20 p.m.

"When do you expect him to be back?' Garrison asked.

"Soon, probably."

"Did he call you on his cell phone? Could you give me his cell number?" Garrison questioned.

"No. He called from his office. He doesn't have a cell phone," she replied.

"I see. Just out of curiosity, does he ever talk about Bridgewater University?"

"It sounds familiar. He may have brought it up in conversation. But if that has something to do with his job, then it would be in passing. He hardly ever talks about his work. He tells me he's not allowed to discuss patients," she answered.

"So Bridgewater University has no meaning to you then?" Garrison asked.

"Nope. Not that I can think of. Sometimes he guest lectures, but that's very rare. Maybe he did that there. It's just a guess," she responded.

Garrison smiled. "Okay then. Well, when he does get in can you give him my number?"

"Yes. Hold on a second while I get a pen," she said.

"No problem."

"Okay, what is it?"

"It's 555-3456," Garrison answered. "Make sure he calls as soon as he gets in."

"I will," she said. "And you said your name was Garrison, correct?"

"Yes. Agent Hank Garrison."

"And the place you asked me about was Bridgewater University?" she asked.

"Yes it was. You sure it doesn't ring a bell? Anything would be useful right now."

"Bridgewater. Bridgewater. It does sound familiar. He may even have treated some students from there. But like I said, only he would know."

"Okay then. Have a goodnight, ma'am," Garrison said.

"You too."

Garrison hung up the phone.

"Anything?" Billy asked.

"He may have lectured there and he may have treated some students from there. His wife didn't seem too sure of either."

"Well, if he did one or the other, there's a pretty good chance he may be the one we're looking for," Billy said.

"There certainly is a good chance."

Chapter 38

The masked man walked up to the bedroom door. He unlocked it and walked inside.

"Hello, all," the man said cheerily. "How's everyone doing so far? The study is almost on its way. I'm ready to take the first participant now."

Krista stared at the masked man trying to figure out who it could be. The body looked like it could be any male. The voice was too muffled to give anything away and the eyes couldn't be seen. Every inch of the man's body was covered. It was impossible to figure out who he was.

She sensed something was wrong.

She was afraid.

"I would like to leave the experiment now," Krista said.

The man tilted his head and looked at her. "Are you sure you want to do that? You do know that you will fail the study, right?"

"Yes," she replied.

"No, she wants to stay," Kenny said. "She's just a little scared right now."

Krista hit Kenny hard. "No, I am serious. I want to go."

"I could have you wait in the van until it's all over. We do have to leave here all together. You don't have to stay here if you don't want to, but there really isn't anywhere to go, except the van," the man said.

"I can call for a ride," she replied.

The man nodded his head. "Okay then." He looked around the room at the faces of the students. "Anyone else want to fail this experiment and join her?"

No one answered.

"Krista, are you sure you want to do this?" Kenny asked.

"Ken, just let her go," Travis said.

"Yes, I'm sure."

The man grabbed Krista gently by the arm and walked her out of the room. He turned to the group of students. I will bring her to the van and then I will be back for experiment number one."

"Can you not lock the door this time?" Perry asked.

"Oh, did I lock it? I'm sorry about that," he said.

The door shut as he left the room.

"Well, at least we know this whole thing is real," Kenny said. "Otherwise he wouldn't have taken Krista to the van."

"Whatever," Travis replied. "I'm going back downstairs and grabbing some sandwiches. You coming with?"

"Yeah, I'll join you," Kenny answered.

Travis walked to the door and grabbed the knob.

Still locked.

* * *

"So why don't you want to do the experiment?" the man asked Krista.

"It's just not worth it. I have a good enough grade. You've scared me enough, if that was your intention. If the experiment was to scare us, you win. You got me. I'm too freaked out right now," she answered.

"That seems hardly true," he said as he reached into his jacket pocket.

"Why is that?" she asked.

"Because I'd be more afraid to be left in a van alone than to be inside a room with my friends."

Krista didn't get to respond as the brunt of the gun handle hit her hard over the head. She fell to the floor.

Unconscious.

"Weird. I never thought anything could really knock someone out with just one blow."

He looked down at Krista's limp body. Blood dripped from her head down the side of her face.

The man quickly walked into the kitchen and opened up some drawers.

Nothing useful.

He opened up a cabinet and grabbed a roll of duct tape.

"This will have to do," he said.

He walked back over to Krista's body and put her feet together and wrapped them securely with the tape. He took her hands and put them behind her back and wrapped them together, too.

Krista started to wake up. Her head picked up off the floor. She was in a daze.

The man pushed her head back to the floor with great force. He then started wrapping the tape around her mouth.

She tried to move her hands and legs, but it was of

no use. She couldn't scream either. The tape muffled her cries. It stifled her screams.

It didn't block her fears though.

The man grabbed Krista's taped up legs and pulled her down the stairs. Her head hit each step hard.

One.

Two.

Three.

Four.

Five.

He opened up the small closet and then stood Krista up next to it. She was in a lot of pain. Too hurt to try to escape. But it would be pointless anyhow.

He stuffed her inside the closet and forcefully shut the door.

He knocked on the door. "There's no knob inside of there so sit pretty until I get to you. You shouldn't have backed out. You would have had a better chance if you didn't. Just be glad you're not claustrophobic."

***

"So what do you say we just jump out the window?" Perry asked as he looked out of the window, down to the ground below. "It's only about thirty feet or so."

"Are you serious?" Travis asked. "You're weight would end up killing you."

"Guys, let's seriously look into what's going on here. Think about it, so what if we're locked in here," Kenny said.

"So what? That seems a bit strange. We're locked

inside a room with a masked man outside doing God only knows what," Perry replied.

"I know it seems weird to us right now, but let's be rational about the whole thing. This is an experiment. This could very well be the whole experiment. His object is to scare us. I have to admit it is a little bit strange, but this is Bridgewater, guys. This isn't the slums of New York," Kenny said. "What do you expect to happen?"

"I hope you're right, Kenny," Perry answered.

"Hey, all I know is I'm not scared," Travis started. "That man can do all he wants and I won't budge. I won't shake and I won't shiver. This is reality, not some lame ass scary movie. Kenny is right. This seems all too unreal right now, but I think that's his point. He wants us to be afraid. I won't let him get the pleasure."

Travis looked at the light switch and flicked it off.

"Hey, asshole, turn on the friggin' light," Sara shouted as the group was lost in darkness.

Travis let out an evil sounding laugh.

Kenny flicked on the light switch. "Travis, grow up."

"I was just testing everyone." Travis looked at the short, chubby girl standing across the room. "Seeing if anyone was afraid of the dark."

Chapter 39

Garrison was about to read from the transcript but stopped and looked at Billy.

"Where's the tape the murderer left us?" Garrison asked.

"Last I heard it was in one of the viewing rooms to see if anything went unnoticed," Billy answered.

Garrison stood up. "Well, I think we should watch it again for ourselves. We have to analyze everything. There's something we aren't seeing yet. I want to find out what it is."

Billy stayed seated. "Shouldn't we wait until Nickerson calls first?"

"What for? I don't have to be in my office to get his call. I gave his wife my cell number," Garrison said as he walked out of the office.

"Oh, I'm sorry." Billy got up and followed.

"What do you think was overlooked on the tape? The transcript is word for word," Billy said.

"Oh, I know it is, but there's something that is

much more real in viewing the tape than reading what was on it. Sometimes it's not what you say, but how you say it," Garrison replied.

They reached one of the viewing rooms and walked inside. Garrison looked at a stack of videos atop one of the televisions and pulled out the one marked *The Rose Murders*.

"Here we go," he said as he put it into the VCR and turned on the television.

The two men stood in front of the television with their arms crossed as the video played.

'If you are watching this then you have somehow found your way to the crime scene. Maybe people were reported missing. Maybe a neighbor heard some shots. I hardly care about the reasons as to why you may be here, because the fact of the matter is that you are here now.'

Garrison paused the video and looked at Billy. "What information did they find out on the neighbor who reported the gunshots?"

"He told the police he heard gunshots from a neighboring house. The house was secluded. He didn't see anyone or see any car. He told them that he wasn't even sure where the shots were fired. Just that they sounded close by. The neighbor's house was a good quarter mile from the rented out one," Billy answered. "Didn't someone tell you this?"

"No. I knew about the reported gunshots, but not about all that other stuff. It must have been in the write-up, but I've been too stressed to look at everything in the folder. I've basically been just staring at the transcript the whole time. Something that leads us to him is right in this video. I know that. So the neighbor didn't see any vehicle?"

"No. He reported the gunshots and that's all."

"Okay." Garrison pressed the 'play' button on the VCR.

'*I must say I deserve a round of applause from all who are viewing this. You will get a very good reading on who I am, but I doubt you will find me.*'

He pressed the pause button again. "A very good reading on who I am. What does that sound like to you? The 'good reading' part."

"Some psychology babble," Billy answered.

"In a way. But I get a different feeling," Garrison responded.

"What would that be?"

"Psychiatrists read people, but they aren't the ones being read."

"And that means?" Billy asked.

"It means he may not be a psychiatrist. He may be a patient," Garrison answered.

"Wow, you really do analyze things. Maybe *you* should be a psychiatrist."

Garrison pressed the 'play' button.

If you do I will congratulate you. And I must say I will go easy. I will not fight. In fact, perhaps I want you to find me. But that's the fun of all this. It's more difficult than you think. I'm getting ahead of myself though. So let me just get to what you are all waiting for. The bodies. I must admit they were all useful guinea pigs. This was an experiment worth a thorough description. This was a lesson worth teaching.'

Garrison paused the tape again. "But this is different," he said. "This implies a teacher. A 'lesson' must refer to teaching something. This would lead us to think it's Miles."

"He's playing with us," Billy said.

"Yes he is. In a way, we're his guinea pigs," Garrison replied. "It's like he wants to see what we will do in the situation he put us in."

Chapter 40

The man stood in front of the bedroom door. He reached into his pocket and pulled out the papers with the fears written on them. He pulled out Perry's paper and then stuffed the others back into his pocket. He reached into another pocket and pulled out the notes he wrote down and flipped through them until he found the one he was looking for. Once he picked it out, he put it with the one with Perry's name and put the others back in his pocket.

He unlocked the door and entered the room.

"Why did you lock the damn door again?" Travis asked as soon as the man walked in.

"I'm sorry once again," the man apologized.

"Sorry doesn't cut it. We don't want to be locked in here like a bunch of lunatics. We came here for a study not for this shit," Travis replied, trying to sound cool in front of the others.

"I will no longer lie to you. This is all part of the study. It's how you handle yourself in stressful situations. You would call this stressful, now wouldn't you? I wasn't supposed to give out the secret, but now that you know maybe I should fail you all," the man said.

"No, don't do that because of this shithead," Sara said pointing to Travis. "Some of us aren't complaining."

"We've already had one failure, would you like to be the next to walk away with an 'F'?" the man asked Travis.

"No," Travis answered.

"Okay then. Now that that is settled, you still all must deal with me locking the door when I leave. The experiment is about to begin. Which one of you is Perry?" the man asked.

Perry walked towards the masked man. "That would be me."

"Good. Okay then, just come with me. You'll be first."

Perry walked out of the room and the man closed the door and locked it.

***

"And the plot thickens," Travis joked.

"Why did you say all that stuff when he came in here?" Kenny asked.

"I don't know. Maybe try to scare him. Reverse the roles a little," Travis answered.

"What if he actually is Miles or some other professor? I don't think talking to a professor like that will sit very well when the grading process takes place," Kenny said.

"I could give a rat's ass who the hell he is. He can't

fail me because I asked why he locked the door," Travis replied.

"Kenny, who do *you* think he is?" Sara asked.

"I have no clue. I'd guess a professor, but I don't know how these studies go," Kenny responded.

"I spoke with Miles earlier today and he said they are conducted by students or professors," Sara said.

"Did he say he was doing this one?" Kenny asked.

"No. He said he wasn't," Sara said.

"So then, it could be another professor," Kenny replied.

"Or a student," Sara added.

"I really love this back and forth banter you two are having," Travis sarcastically said. "Can the rest of us join in on this guessing game? Help pass the time?"

***

"So, Perry, are you having fun so far?" the man asked as he walked into the kitchen.

"Well, not exactly. I think if you were in our shoes you wouldn't be having much fun either," Perry answered.

"You make a good point, my friend. So let the experiment begin." The man reached into his pocket and pulled out a gun.

Chapter 41

Garrison and Billy watched some more of the video.

'Victim number one. The male killed in the bathroom. His task was simple. All he had to do was last twenty minutes without washing his hands. I'd have let him go free if he was able to wait a measly twenty minutes. Too bad. He seemed like a nice guy. Charismatic, kind, a real go-getter. But he was impatient. He had to learn his lesson. If you're all wondering why the faucet was left running, well let me fill you in on a little secret. It was running even before I put him in the room. He never turned it on, but he did use it. Sad to say, too. He only lasted a whole ten minutes and fourteen seconds. You can check for prints on the faucet, but I don't think you'll find any. Trust me.'

Garrison pressed pause. "This stuff we already figured out. The victim had OCD. That would explain the running faucet. It also gives meaning to 'impatient.'"

"You say that because he must have been impatient because of his OCD, right? Nothing deeper than that," Billy said.

Garrison smiled. "Yes, that's the only reason. Although I could be a little more analytical and say that maybe he slipped it in there to have a play on words with 'patient.' That would mean we're back to Nickerson being the number one suspect. Nickerson or one of his patients."

"I hope you're not serious," Billy responded.

"I'm not. But it does make a bit of sense," Garrison said.

"It's a stretch."

Garrison pressed the 'play' button.

'Victim number two. The female killed in the bedroom. Her task was also simple. All I wanted to know was whether or not her dilemma, her illness some might say, was real. Perhaps it could be fixed. A gun aimed at her head would be a worthy way to fix it. Who can sleep with such a thing on their mind? Who can sleep worrying about dying? I know I wouldn't be able to. Apparently she could. But don't worry it was painless. I assure you, she didn't feel a thing. We all grow up wanting to die in our sleep anyhow. She got her wish. She only lasted five hours. Funny to think about that. Could you last only five hours with a gun aimed at you?'

Garrison didn't bother to pause the tape. "Nothing peculiar there."

'Victim number three. The female killed in the kitchen. I believe her task was the simplest of the three. It was also my favorite. I'll be the first to admit that some of us love food while others don't, but she happened to be way out there in the food department.'

Garrison paused the tape. "Why was it his favorite? Was he bulimic, too? Did he suffer from an eating disorder?"

"Maybe," Billy said. "But he doesn't look very thin in the video. He looks pretty big, actually."

"It's probably all the layers he's wearing. He may not be very big at all. But he could be. It's another one of those 'who knows?'"

Garrison played the tape.

'She was thin; a nice athletic physique. I'd pay a pretty penny for someone like her to strip for me. Hell, I'd pay a pretty dime. Unfortunately, it was worthless. She could have lived. All she had to do was last a mere thirty-two minutes. Have a good home cooked meal, which I assure you was not poisoned, and relax. Apparently her gag reflex got the best of her. It's quite a shame. Only lasted twenty minutes. By the way, you won't find any utensils, no forks or knives, no spoons either. She had to eat with her hands. Putting her fingers in her mouth. Easy job for most. Not for her, I guess.'

'I'm sure you've found my three roses among the wreckage. Let's make this number four. It's a rarity, you know. It won't happen again. Well, death may happen again, but the roses won't. You only get four. You have to figure out what that means. Are they meaningful at all?'

Garrison paused the tape. "There's the key right there. The roses. We need to figure out what they mean. Why only four? Why is it a rarity?"

"It's a pretty strange riddle," Billy answered.

Garrison pressed the 'play' button.

'I suppose only time will tell. Only time will indicate whether you failed or did not fail. Time is what we're all looking for more of, but when we get it we don't know how to use it properly. So sometimes it's best just

to wait things out. Sometimes you're trying to figure out what has just happened won't work. Sometimes it needs to figure out you. Until we meet again.'

The video went black and Garrison turned off the television.

"Only time will tell." Garrison slowly shook his head. "Time."

Chapter 42

A good ten minutes had passed since Perry had been taken out of the bedroom. The students waited patiently for their turn in the experiment. Most were still a little skeptical, but they wanted to get the whole thing over with. If the experiment was solely to scare those who participated in it, then it certainly was working.

When the door finally opened, the five students who remained locked inside immediately turned to see who the visitor would be.

Either Perry returning to tell how his experiment went or the strange masked man?

The masked man rang victorious.

He walked inside and looked at everyone in the room. One by one he stared at them.

He was looking for his next victim.

He pulled out a piece of paper from his pocket and glanced down at it. His hand was shaking a bit. His whole body looked like it was trembling. He looked around at the students again.

"Where's Perry?" Kenny asked.

The masked man just shook his head.

"Shane Davis," was all the man uttered.

A short, skinny guy from within the group of five walked closer to the man. "That would be me. Am I next?"

The man just nodded. He motioned his hand out the door and Shane walked out of the room.

"Is Perry finished? Can you send him back in here?" Kenny asked.

The man shook his head and shut the door as he walked out of the room.

He made sure the door was locked.

***

"He could have at least told us how Perry's experiment went," Kenny said.

"It doesn't seem like he talks much, kind of like the kid he just took, so it's almost pointless to ask him anything," Travis replied. "But I'm sure Perry is sitting pretty, eating some more food downstairs, just waiting for us to join him. At least if he doesn't eat everything first."

"I don't understand why he wouldn't just come back and stay with us though," Sara said.

Kenny shrugged. "Maybe he would reveal too much about the study. Maybe if he returned to the room he'd tell us how easy the whole thing was and we wouldn't be afraid any longer, thus defeating the whole point of this study."

"I guess you're right. That does make sense," Sara answered.

"By the way, Sara, I have been meaning to ask Krista something, but it looks as if that will have to wait," Kenny said.

"What is it?" Sara asked.

"I wanted to know what she's doing for Spring Break. Do you know? Has she told you anything?"

"You still haven't told her?" Travis asked.

Kenny looked at Travis then turned back to Sara. "So do you know?"

"Yeah. We've been talking about it the past couple of days. My parents got us tickets for a cruise," Sara replied.

"Oh." Kenny sounded disappointed.

"What are you going to do?" Sara asked.

Kenny turned to Travis and then looked at Sara again. "We're taking a road trip. I was going to have you two join us, but obviously a cruise is much more fun."

Sara smiled. "Yeah, sorry. Well, the open sea and the open road. They both will be fun, I'm sure."

"Us guys," Travis started as he put his arm around Kenny's shoulder and smiled, "will have a blast."

***

Shane followed the masked man down into the cellar.

"Is this where the experiment is? It's kind of cold and dark. Can you turn on a light?" Shane asked.

The man reached for the string that turns on the light bulb. He grabbed the small string and pulled it. The light went on.

Shane looked around the cellar. He shivered as he saw a few spiders crawl on the walls and across the floor. The cellar was crowded with bugs of all kinds.

"Can we please do this somewhere else?" Shane asked in a jumpy voice.

The man shook his head.

"I don't think I can do any type of experiment down here. Can we go upstairs?"

The man shook his head again.

Out of the corner of his eye Shane could see a large spider dart across the room.

He closed his eyes and his face tensed up. He shivered again.

The masked man reached inside of his pocket and pulled out two pieces of paper.

Shane's eyes were moving from one part of the room to the other, darting nervously back and forth from one bug to the next. He observed every spider and insect that paraded around the cellar.

Shane didn't even look at the man. His eyes were focused at everything else that was happening around him. "Please, can we do this somewhere else?" he asked.

The masked man pushed Shane hard. It caught Shane by surprise and he fell to the floor. His head hit the concrete ground hard. He was stunned at what had just happened and when he sat up he noticed one of the spiders was close by.

The man put his hand into his jacket pocket.

Shane shivered at the close encounter with the large, hairy brown spider and shot right back to his feet. He turned to the masked man.

"Why did…." He couldn't finish his sentence as he slowly took a step backward.

166

A gun was aimed at his head. The man's hands were trembling, but it was Shane who was scared.

Shane took another step back. He heard a loud crunch as his shoe squashed a large spider.

He shivered again as he looked down at the yellow goo. He shivered even more when he looked at the masked man's gun.

He wanted to run, but he was afraid he'd be shot. He didn't know whether or not this was real, he half-heartedly believed the discussions in the bedroom about the whole thing being just an experiment to test one's fear. But he couldn't chance it. He was too afraid. He was slowly being backed into a corner.

Shane took another step back, but realized he was just making it easier for the man to corner him. He gradually turned his head and saw a large spider web just a few inches from his face. He shivered again.

The man stepped closer to him. Shane stayed where he was.

The man stepped closer still. He was now just an arm's length away from Shane.

"What do you want from me? What is all this about? I don't want to be part of this experiment anymore," Shane said trembling with fear.

The man held out the two pieces of paper he had retrieved from his pocket. The gun was still aimed at his head.

"Here," the man said shaking the papers at Shane.

Shane stood still.

"Here," the man repeated.

Shane slowly took the papers from the man. His hands were shaking uncontrollably.

"This is your experiment," the man said.

Shane looked down at the two sheets of paper. The first was the one he had written on the ride to the house.
Shane Davis
Spiders

The second was something he hadn't seen before.
EXPERIMENT #2: The arachnophobic. So why are you afraid of spiders? Do they creep you out? They are scary little creatures, aren't they? Some may be crawling on you right now. Did you know we all eat about eight in our lifetime? Quite the bit of knowledge. I doubt you really cared to know that. The experiment I would like to conduct on you is to see just how afraid of spiders you truly are. There are things I fear, but I must say that bugs aren't one of them. If you want to live, you'll conquer your fear of spiders. I mean, really, what's creepier- spiders or a gun to the head? You decide. The experiment is simple, if you want to live. It really is. All you have to do is find a spider web and stick your head in it. Face first, of course. But there's a catch. There always is. You must let a few crawl across your face. Their long, hairy legs must make their way around your head. Sounds scary, I know, especially for you. I know the feeling; it makes you all tingly inside. You tremble and shiver at just the image. But you can't tremble or shiver this time. If you even flinch, you will be shot. I assure you of that. And if you're wondering if the gun is real, I wouldn't even try to test it. One minute, Mr. Davis. Just one minute is all it takes for your survival. Good luck!

Shane dropped the papers. He was shivering more than ever. The thought of dying or facing spiders were almost equal to him.

Shane looked at the man. "Why this? Why are you doing this?"

The man pointed to the spider web behind Shane.

Shane closed his eyes. He tried to fight back the images. He was trembling from the thoughts of both death and spiders. If the man were telling the truth, if the gun was real, he'd have to stop trembling. He hadn't even had a spider crawl on him yet and he already had had enough.

The image of a large spider crawling across his face gave him the chills.

"Please stop trembling and do what the paper says," the man said looking around the room. "If you keep trembling I'm going to have to shoot you."

The comment just made Shane more afraid. He couldn't stop his body from shaking.

It was impossible.

The man reached into a nearby web and grabbed a spider from it. He held it in his gloved hand. "They aren't that bad." The spider crawled across the man's hand.

Shane didn't look at it. He was still trying to pretend they didn't even exist. He was trying to pretend everything was a dream.

"Please stop shaking. You only have so long," the man said. "Don't flinch when I put this on you. Don't even close your eyes. This is life or death." The man waited until the spider was in the center of his palm and then closed his hand into a loose fist. He walked one step closer to Shane and put his closed hand atop Shane's shoulder. "Do not flinch."

The man opened up his hand and the large spider fell out.

Shane couldn't stop his body from jumping. He flailed his arms and swiped the spider off his shoulder.

The man shivered slightly and then looked around the room again before turning to the trembling Shane.

"I'm sorry," the man said. "You failed."

He pulled the trigger. An almost silent gunshot erupted.

The silencer was on. Assuring that no one heard the sound upstairs.

Shane fell to the floor.

Blood slowly dripped out of the bullet wound and painted the concrete ground. One of the numerous spiders on the ground crept up his lifeless face.

Chapter 43

Garrison and Billy were back in the office. Garrison pulled out the transcript again, by now he almost had it all memorized.

"We just saw the video and now you want to read it?" Billy asked.

"This is how it's done, Billy. You haven't been an agent long enough to understand all this. This is your first big case. I can't sleep at night because I have death on my mind all the time. Until I know who this bastard is I won't be able to sleep again," Garrison answered.

Billy nodded.

"We're still missing so much. He's got a big jump on us and we've got so little on him," Garrison said. He looked down at the paper and the time limit of the experiments. "These times, these numbers, are important. They'll lead us to something."

He looked at how long each victim lasted. "The male victim lasted ten minutes, about half of what he was supposed to. The woman with narcolepsy lasted five hours, about a quarter of what she was supposed to do. And the woman in the kitchen lasted twenty minutes, just twelve minutes shy of her time," Garrison said.

"So?" Billy asked.

"Well." Garrison rubbed his forehead and huffed. "Why those times? He also refers to the victims in order," Garrison stopped and pulled out a sheet from the folder, "but it says in the report that the woman in the bedroom was the last to die. She was victim number two. The report also claims that Hartnett and Montgomery, victims one and three, were killed at around the same time period. Around three to six hours prior to victim two."

"Well, that makes sense, she did last the longest," Billy said.

"I know that, but why list them by victim number if he didn't kill them in that order? And how could he have killed two people at the same time?" Garrison questioned.

"Maybe there was more than one killer, like I said before. Like you told me you had originally thought," Billy replied.

Garrison's face lit up. "Not necessarily," he said as he looked down at the report. "Remember how the bathroom and bedroom doors were locked?"

Billy nodded. "Yes."

"Well, the kitchen didn't have a door. The girl in the kitchen must have been the first to have been killed," Garrison said.

"Why do you say that?" Billy asked.

"Because the others were locked away. They couldn't have escaped. She would have been able to," Garrison responded.

"But what about the time limit? How did he know how long the others lasted if he was with the girl in the kitchen?" Billy asked.

"I knew you would ask that. I think he probably started experiment three, the woman in the kitchen, first. He watched over her until she failed. She was shot and then he started on experiment one, the victim in the bathroom. After that one was done he moved on to victim two," Garrison answered.

"Isn't that risky? Without someone keeping an eye on the others locked in the rooms, who knew what they could have done. They may have tried to escape through a window or something," Billy said.

"Maybe they were too scared. Or maybe they were too comfortable. If they still believed it was a study, it's possible they just waited. But I think I found a different route," Garrison replied.

"And what route would that be?" Billy asked.

Garrison picked up a piece of paper from his desk and handed it to Billy. "Look at this."

Billy looked at the message on the paper.
Professor Randall Miles
Psychology Department
Bridgewater University
Office 312

Billy looked back at Garrison. "You think the professor killed them?"

"Look at his office number," Garrison instructed.

Billy looked at the paper again. "Okay, office 312."

"Remember how I said numbers would be important?" Garrison asked.

"Yes."

"Well experiments one, two, and three, may have been done in the order I just told you. The order of three, one, and then two. Three twelve. The professor's office number," Garrison said.

Chapter 44

"I wish I would have brought some of my books to this thing. I could have studied and done homework while I waited," Kenny said. "This is taking longer than expected."

"Yeah, I mean, the least this guy could have done was leave some magazines in this room. I mean, if we're going to be locked inside of here, we might as well have some good reading material," Travis said.

"So you are comparing this to a dentist's office, huh? Like you want some educational magazines just lying around on a desk?" Kenny questioned.

"Sort of. I mean, I was thinking more along the lines of some pornographic shit, but anything would do good right about now. I mean, let alone we're stuck in here, but I have to listen to you whine about Krista," Travis said.

"Oh shut up," Kenny replied.

Travis continued as he looked at Sara, "I have to listen to you talk about how rich you are." He turned to the chubby girl. "And I have to listen to you breath because you haven't uttered a word since you got in here."

"You are so rude," Kenny said. "It's almost like you want to start trouble. No one in here has said one thing to you and this is how you act towards them?"

***

The masked man walked back up to the bedroom, trembling from what he had just done.

Or shaking with excitement.

He unlocked the door and entered the room. Now four people stared back at him.

He pulled out two pieces of paper from his pocket and looked at the students.

"This is taking too long. You've only done two experiments so far and we've been here for almost an hour. By the time you're finished we'll have been here for far longer than you told us. We signed up for this because it was quick and easy. Why has it become something so different?" Kenny asked.

The man didn't answer the question. He looked down at the papers.

"Madison Rowe."

The chubby, baby-faced girl walked up to the man. "That's me."

The man showed her the way out the door and followed behind her. He locked the door as soon as he shut it.

"Follow me," he said as he walked down the steps.

Madison followed the man. "Where are we going?" she asked.

The man stopped on the last step just before the

concrete cellar floor.

He pointed to the dark room.

Madison looked ahead, her face a bit panicked. "Can you turn on the light so I can see where I'm going?"

The man shook his head. He put his hand in his pocket and grabbed the gun.

Madison looked at the weapon in disbelief. She tried to run up the stairs, but the man grabbed her leg and she tripped. She fell face first onto a step, cutting her lip.

The man walked up to the step her head was on and grabbed her neck. He pushed her face hard against the cold step. "Read this," he said as he put a piece of paper in front of her eyes. The gun was now pressed upon her temple.

Madison was trembling in fear. She was still in shock at what was happening. It all happened so quickly. She didn't have enough time to get away.

She looked at the paper in front of her.

Experiment #3: The girl who's afraid of the dark. What is it that makes the absence of light so scary? Is it that you do not know what is lurking inside the dark or is it something far greater? Does a boogeyman lurk in our closets or underneath our beds once the lights get turned off? Does violence only occur at night when the moonlight isn't enough to scare away criminals? Why are you afraid of the dark? It's not what you don't see that should scare you; it's what you can see. It's what is right in front of your eyes. Perhaps the gun to the back of your head or the inevitable death that will come upon each and every one of us. Why are you afraid of the dark if once you die you will be stuck in darkness forever? The experiment is easy; at least I think it is. No boogeyman lurks in this cellar, not unless you include me. All you have to do is make your way from one end of the darkened cellar to the other. If you can do that you will be set free. You will have passed the experiment. Just don't scream. Good luck!

"Do the experiment and you'll be fine," the man said. "Please pass the test."

The man walked a few steps in front of Madison. "No sneaky business," he said. "Do the experiment and you will be set free." He kept the gun aimed at Madison's head.

She slowly got up off the steps and walked down them. The man followed her. She was shaking wildly.

"Don't scream," he said.

She took one step at a time.

She was almost to the other side. Her foot hit something hard and she stumbled and fell to the floor.

"You're almost there," the man said. "Touch the wall and you'll be okay. Trust me. Just don't scream."

Madison was now on her hands and knees. She slowly crawled a little further; she could not see where she was going. Her head bumped into something.

It was the wall.

She had reached the end.

She had completed the experiment.

"I did it," she said in a scared whisper.

"Good job." The man pulled on the light bulb string. "Don't scream."

Madison squinted as her eyes adjusted to the bright lights.

When she was finally able to see again, she looked

down at her hands. They were covered in blood. She slowly spun around from the wall and looked at the ground.

Shane's body was just a few inches away from her.

She wanted to scream, but feared she would be shot for doing so. She began to hyperventilate.

Out of the corner of her eye she saw something else in the cellar.

She was paralyzed with fear.

The light bulb flickered and then popped. Darkness engulfed the room again.

Madison screamed in horror.

A gunshot went off creating a brief, bright flash among the cellar's darkness.

Chapter 45

"There's still no answer," Garrison said as he hung up the phone.

"So what do you suggest we do?" Billy asked.

Garrison got up from his chair. "Break down his door and see what he has inside."

"Are you serious?" Billy asked in shock. "This doesn't seem like you. An hour ago you didn't even want to go to visit Miles."

"An hour ago we had nothing on him. Now we do," Garrison replied.

"So an office number later and you think you have something? Are you serious?" Billy questioned again.

"Of course I'm serious. You said it's only twenty minutes away from here. We have to see where this leads us," Garrison replied.

Billy shot up from his seat. "Let's go then."

Garrison walked out of his office and Billy followed right behind. Just before Garrison reached the building's exit he stopped.

"What is it? A change of heart?" Billy asked.

"I have to get the case folder," Garrison answered. "You can drive while I see if there is anything that's missing. I don't want to jump to conclusions. That's what he wants us to do. If we go to Miles' house we may be wasting time."

"Wow, Hank, you really jump back and forth. First you don't want to go there, then you do, and now you're not sure," Billy said.

"It's true, Billy, I just don't know what's right anymore. Sometimes something looks so good and then within minutes something looks better."

"But we are going to see Miles', right? I mean, even if it may be jumping to conclusions, even if we may be wasting time, it's better than regretting that we didn't do it. There's still a good chance he's the one," Billy replied.

"I know. Hold on a minute while I run back and get the folder."

Garrison hurried back to his office and looked at all the papers on his desk. He shoved them all inside the folder and walked out of his office.

The sheets of papers weren't securely inside the folder and a few slipped out.

One fluttered to the ground and landed at Garrison's feet. He bent over to pick it up and the words on the sheet seemed to be beckoning him.

Jeffrey Thompson, the neighbor who was renting out the closest house to the crime scene, called the police at 2:10 p.m. to report hearing three gunshots off in the distance. Police arrived at the scene at 2:21 p.m. Thompson did not see any suspicious happenings over at the house, which was a quarter of a mile away from his own.

Garrison stopped reading. "How could that be?" he asked himself.

He walked back into his office and placed the folder on his desk then fumbled through the pages and found the transcript. He looked it over.

"That doesn't make sense," he said. "The gunshots would have been too far apart to have reported three. One would make sense, maybe two. But not three. One victim was shot long after the other two."

Garrison left the papers on his desk and walked out of his office and back to Billy.

"What took so long?" Billy asked. He looked at Garrison. "And where is the folder?"

"We can't go yet," Garrison replied.

Billy gave a puzzled look. "Why not?"

"I found something else. I'm surprised I hadn't noticed it sooner," Garrison answered.

"What is it?" Billy asked.

Garrison took a deep breath then exhaled loudly. "The neighbor reported the three gunshots. He's the one who led the police to the crime scene."

"That's right," Billy said.

"But doesn't that seem a bit strange?" Garrison asked.

"Not really. He heard gunshots, got worried, and called the police. What's so strange about that?"

"Three people were killed. That means three gunshots went off. But they didn't go off all at once or one after the other. Each victim was shot at different times. That means that it would be strange to call after all the shots had gone off. There could have been hours between the three. The woman killed in the bedroom wasn't shot until five hours had passed. No one would have waited that long to report gunshots," Garrison replied.

Billy nodded. "Yes, that would be strange."

"Of course. The neighbor wanted the police to come to the crime scene. It was his intent to get them there. He wanted them to find his experiment. If he hadn't called then it may have taken a long time until they even found the house. It was secluded to begin with," Garrison said.

"What was the neighbor's name?" Billy asked.

"Jeffrey Thompson, but that doesn't matter. The names aren't real."

Garrison jumped as his cell phone started to vibrate. He took it off its clip on his belt and answered it.

"Agent Garrison," he said.

"Yes; hello, Mr. Garrison. This is Cheryl Nickerson, Philip's wife. I just wanted to let you know that he just called me. I gave him your message."

"I thought he couldn't call you. I thought he didn't have a cell phone," Garrison replied.

"He doesn't. He forgot something in his office and had to turn around and get it. He called me from there," Cheryl answered.

"Why isn't he calling me then?" Garrison asked.

"I don't know. He told me he'd rather talk to you in person. He said he has something you'd be interested in," she responded.

"He's at his office now?"

"Yes. He said he'll stay there until you arrive," she answered.

"Okay." Garrison hung up the phone without saying 'goodbye.'

Billy looked at him. "What was that about?"

"Apparently Dr. Nickerson wants to talk to us in person. He's at his office now," Garrison replied.

"Isn't that a bit odd? What would this be about?"

"His wife said he told her that it was something we'd be interested in," Garrison answered.

"What could it be, aside from a confession?"

"I guess we'll have to see," Garrison replied. "Let's call him and find out."

Chapter 46

Nickerson put his pen down on top of a letter he just finished writing. He opened up one of his drawers and pulled out the article he had been reading earlier in the day and then rummaged through the drawer and pulled out a sheet of paper.

It was crumpled and dirty.

He set them both on the side of his letter and then dropped his head into his hands.

"Too much burden. Too much trouble," he muttered.

'Ring. Ring. Ring.'

Nickerson glanced at the ringing phone on his desk and picked it up. He slammed it back on its receiver then unplugged its cord. He looked at the long telephone wire and smirked. "Too much burden."

Nickerson ran his fingers across the wire until it reached the back of the phone. He unplugged it from the phone. He wrapped the long wire around his hand and looked up at the small ceiling fan above him.

High enough, he thought. *And sturdy enough, too.*

Nickerson got off his chair and walked over to his closet. He looked inside and grabbed a metal foldout chair and opened it up. He placed the chair a few inches from his desk.

Nickerson stepped onto the chair. It wobbled a bit before stabilizing.

He unraveled the wire from his hand. It was so tightly wrapped around his fingers that they had become engorged with blood and were turning red. He wrapped one end of the wire around the ceiling fan and securely tied it. He then wrapped the other end around his neck and tied it tightly. His face was quickly beginning to turn colors.

Nickerson pulled at the wire to check its strength. "Good."

He started to sway side to side on the metal chair. The chair wobbled uncontrollably until it finally fell over. Nickerson was hanging in the air.

He instinctively pulled at the tightening wire across his neck, but it hardly did anything.

He was losing air and his face was turning blue.

All of a sudden the wire snapped and Nickerson fell to the floor.

He breathed heavily and reached for the wire around his neck. He unraveled it quickly. His face slowly returned to its normal shade.

"Shit!" he said.

Nickerson shot up from the floor and walked back to his desk and opened up the drawers.

Nothing.

"Damn it!" He looked at the black plastic container that held his pens and pencils. He emptied its contents onto his desk. Nothing.

He quickly glanced around the room, but wound up looking right back at his desk. A silver letter opener had caught his eye. He thought about the cut marks on Troy's arms. He grabbed it off his desk and sat down in his chair.

Nickerson placed the letter opener on his wrist and ran it vertically across his veins. It just scratched the surface lightly. The skin had not been pierced.

He pushed harder.

No use.

He sighed and threw the letter opener to the ground.

Nickerson spun his chair around and looked at the vase full of roses. "Good."

He grabbed the vase and slammed it to the ground. It shattered into many pieces.

Nickerson reached over to pick up one of the sharper pieces of glass. He pricked the tip of his finger with it as a test. The small hole on his finger bled.

He brought the glass towards his wrist and pressed it hard against the skin. It quickly pierced the skin. He dug it in deeper. The skin tore open and the blood poured out rapidly. Nickerson turned to his other wrist and did the same. He dropped the glass on the floor in pain.

His hands dropped over the chair's armrests. Blood dripped down his wrists and into his hands then slowly down his fingers until they finally splattered on the floor below. Some droplets added even more red to the roses scattered among the ground.

Nickerson closed his eyes as he waited for the blood to run dry.

He waited for his life to depart him.

Chapter 47

"So I guess it's just you and me," Travis said as Sara departed the room with the man.

"Sadly," Kenny replied. "You have been nothing other than complete and utterly humiliating tonight. Both to me and to yourself. You're my friend, Travis, and I have to deal with the repercussions that our friendship entails. People like to group friends together, you know? If you act foolish then it makes me seem foolish to be hanging out with you. For all I know, Krista has been indifferent towards me lately because of you."

"Well, if that's true, Kenny, then you shouldn't be with her in the first place. Bros before hoes, you know that. I mean, if Krista can't understand that you're nothing like me, then she obviously doesn't know you well enough," Travis answered.

"I hope she doesn't think I'm like you," Kenny said. "But by you acting like this to her friends, like Sara, you're only making it more difficult for me."

"It's not like you like Sara either. You must admit,

we'd be better off without her. You'd be better off without her. If anything, *she's* making your time spent with Krista more difficult, not me."

***

The masked man brought Sara into the room with the table full of food.

"So where is everyone else?" she asked.

The man pointed outside.

"Isn't it a bit cold to have people be outside until we're finished in here?"

The man shook his head. "Not for them."

"Okay then, let's get this over with. I want my 'A', I have a feeling this will boost my grade up a lot. His tests are hard and I'm struggling a bit, but this should solve all that. Bring it on. Hit me with your best shot. How you going to scare me?" Sara asked.

The man pointed to one of the nearby chairs. "Sit down."

Sara followed the order and sat in the chair.

The man looked around the room and noticed the duct tape on the floor. He picked it up.

"What's that for?" Sara asked.

The man didn't answer.

"I have to admit that this is one of the strangest experiments I've ever heard of. I don't know much about psychology, but I mean you lock people in a bedroom, you're wearing a mask..."

"And yet you're still waiting to see what it is," the man interrupted.

"Well, yeah. I need a decent grade. I haven't reached my maximum level of fear yet. So far I'm not that afraid. A little freaked out by all this, but not afraid."

The man nodded. "Keep your hands on the armrests, please."

Sara looked puzzled. "Why?"

"Because I'm going to tape you in. It's part of the experiment."

Sara got off the chair. "Nah, that's a bit too creepy."

"Okay, then just sit down. But if you move, you fail," the man replied.

"What?"

"If you move, you fail. It's part of the experiment," he answered.

Sara sat back down. "All I have to do is sit still and I pass?"

The man nodded. He put his hand in his jacket pocket and pulled out a piece of paper. "Read this."

The man handed the paper to Sara. He stuck his hand in his pocket again and pulled out the gun.

Sara started to get up off the chair. "Sit down. You move, you fail," the man said with the gun aimed at her head. "Read the paper. What you have to do isn't that hard."

Sara's eyes were tearing up as she looked down at the paper.

Experiment #4: The girl who's afraid of blood. This will be quite the test for you. Bloodshed has occurred on numerous occasions already. But you haven't seen it. What exactly are you afraid of? Watching others die? Watching others get cut open? Or watching yourself die? Does the thought of blood only scare you when it is your own or when it is the blood of others, too? Think for a minute on this. If you want to pass the test you cannot fear the bloodshed. You cannot fear the gore. If you do, then the blood will be dripping from you. All you have to do is stay seated and watch a little blood and a little gore. I'm sure you'll be able to do it. Mind over matter. But if you try to get up, if you try to look away, if you cringe just a little, even if you close your eyes for too long- you will die. The blood that drips will be all yours.

Sara's hands were trembling. Her whole body was shaking. She didn't even finish reading the note. She looked back down.

The task is simple, really. Just watch as the girl who is afraid of the dark bleeds. Watch as her eyes get pulled from their sockets. If she were alive the pain would be unbearable, and darkness would be seen forever. Luckily she isn't. Good luck!

Sara had tears falling down her face. She wanted to scream or run away, but the fear of being shot was the greatest of all. "Why?" she asked.

The man kept the gun aimed at her head then slowly bowed his head. "I have to. It's my experiment."

He backed towards the front door just a few feet away, still with the gun focused on Sara, and opened it. Sara could try to make a run for it, run up to the bedroom and get Travis and Kenny to help her, but she was too afraid of the outcome.

"If this is the experiment," she said in a trembling voice, "then you've won. I give up. You've scared me enough."

"It's a little too late for that," the man replied from the doorway.

He grabbed Madison's lifeless arms from right outside the front door and dragged her body to within a couple of feet from Sara's chair.

Sara cringed as she saw the lifeless body. *It was real*, she thought. *The experiment was real.*

Sara's tears were unstoppable by now. Her body was convulsing. She quickly looked down at the body again and turned away in disgust. Blood poured from the side of Madison's head. Her eyes were opened wide, still struck with terror.

Full of pain.

The man bent down beside the lifeless body and pulled a spoon from his jacket pocket.

Sara turned her eyes away from the body. She was afraid at what would be done.

"You must look at this," the man said. "Please, just look at this."

Sara was hyperventilating.

"I…I…can't…do…do…do…it."

"Everything will be okay if you just watch. You will have passed," the man said.

Sara didn't believe him.

"I…I…can't…trust…that…that…you…are…telling"

The man interrupted her. "I promise. You pass the experiment and you will be set free. Just pass. Please pass."

Sara had her eyes closed.

"You must look at me do this. You must watch," the man said.

Sara slowly opened her eyes and glanced down at the body.

The man slowly brought the spoon closer to Madison's left eye. His hand was trembling.

Sara couldn't take it. She turned away and shivered at the thought of the eye being spooned from the girl's socket.

The man looked at the shivering Sara and then turned to glance at a nearby window. He shivered himself and then slowly turned back to Sara, suddenly angry. "Watch me do this! Watch or you'll end up like her!"

Sara turned back to the body. The spoon was dug into the corner of the eye. The man stuck it further in until just the handle was seen. "Keep watching," the man said. "Almost done."

He turned the spoon within the socket and it made a disgusting sloshing sound. Sara turned away and started to gag.

"Watch this!" the man screamed.

Sara couldn't turn back. It was too much for her to bear. Her stomach was turning. She felt like she was about to pass out.

She looked down at her legs. They were becoming weak.

"Watch!" the man shouted.

Sara wasn't listening.

The man got up from the body and grabbed Sara's chin with his gloved hand full of blood. Her eyes were tightly shut. He glanced out the window again before turning his attention back to her.

"I'm sorry. You failed," he said as he pulled the gun's trigger.

Chapter 48

"Why hasn't he picked up?" Garrison said in an angry voice. "He tells us to meet him and he won't pick up the phone."

"We're almost there," Billy replied.

"I know, but maybe he isn't there," Garrison said. "Maybe he was the murderer and he called to lead us here so that he could be doing other stuff. The video said something about 'time,' maybe that's what this is for. To try and get us to waste time or to try and make more time for himself."

Billy pulled into the parking space beside another car. "There's still a car here. Maybe it's his."

Garrison quickly opened his door and got out. He hurriedly walked up to the building's entrance and turned the knob.

It opened.

The waiting room was dark, but off in the distance Garrison noticed that there was a light shining in Nickerson's office. "Dr. Nickerson," he started, "we're here."

No answer.

"Dr. Nickerson!" Garrison walked up to the office door. Billy had finally caught up to him and was right behind Garrison at the door.

Garrison knocked on the door and then slowly opened it. "Dr. Nick..." He didn't finish at he stared at the dead body sitting in the chair.

"Holy shit!" Billy shouted.

Garrison walked closer to the body. Nickerson's eyes were glossed over, his face was pale. The life had been drained from him.

Garrison stepped in a puddle of blood. "Call the police and have them get over here."

"Why would he do this?" Billy asked.

Garrison didn't answer as he stared down at the papers on Nickerson's desk.

He picked up the article and read it with amazement.

DYING TO GET RID OF YOUR ILLNESS?
If you are, here's a study that can help you do so.
Failure is not an option. Easy tasks to help
you solve your frustrations. Sleeping disorders,
eating disorders, and anxiety disorders most welcome.
No need to call to set up an arrangement.
If you choose to join meet at Bridgewater
University, outside of the main entrance on February
26th at 8 a.m. Transportation will be provided to the
study site.
Thank you.
Dr. Bert Over

It was the same ad I saw, he thought.

"Nickerson may have been the murderer," Garrison said.

Billy was baffled. "That's why we're here, right? Because we think he did it." He closed his cell phone. "The police are on their way."

Garrison handed the article to Billy.

Garrison looked back down at the desk and picked up another sheet of paper and read it.

My intentions were never to hurt anyone. They have always been to help others. My goal in life was to make people conquer their problems and live a good life. Live a real life. Along the way I seemed to have failed. And that shames me most. I know that I cannot help the world, but I have always wanted to help whoever I could. I did something wrong. I didn't help when I could have. And I must pay for my sins. I guess you could say that I didn't conquer my own problem and I couldn't live with the knowledge of knowing what I did. I couldn't be happy knowing what I did. And because of this I couldn't live a good life and must not live a life at all. It's like the experiment said, I can't live a life of secrecy and I can't live a life in jail. I failed.

The suicide note puzzled Garrison. "This doesn't make sense," he said. "Why go so far just to kill yourself?"

"What is it?" Billy asked. "What are you talking about?"

Garrison read the letter out to Billy.

"Doesn't that seem odd?" Garrison asked.

"In a way, but he did say in the video that he

196

wanted to be caught. That he'd give in if someone found him," Billy answered.

"If someone found him alive, but not dead," Garrison said. He looked down at the desk again.

Just pens and pencils.

"He wrote in the letter that 'it's like the experiment says.' What experiment is he talking about?" Garrison asked.

"The one he conducted," Billy answered.

"No. He passed that experiment. He killed them all. Why does he say that he failed this one?"

Garrison looked on the floor at all the pieces of glass, the roses, and the blood mixed with flower water. A crumpled up paper caught his eye just under the desk. He bent over to pick it up. It was wet and bloody, but the message still remained.

Garrison was stunned at what he was reading.

Experiment #4: The doctor. So you told some of your patients this would be a good study for them to join. Like the nice doctor you are, you even came along with one of them. Unfortunately, it was a mistake. Now you are part of the study. Now you have to pass in order to survive. I can tell you now that you may make it out of here alive, but how long will that last? You have a simple task. All you have to do is see that the bulimic stays calm enough to finish her task with a gun aimed at her head. The tough part is that you'll be holding the gun. Then you must comfort your good friend, and patient, in the locked bathroom and try to have him pass his experiment. Then you have to wait with little miss sleepy head. If they pass, then you've done a job well done. You did what you studied to do and fixed them. If they fail you must shoot them. YOU

MUST SHOOT THEM! Why? Because if you do not, you will be the one to get shot. I'll have a gun, too, so you even try something funny and you can kiss your life goodbye. The experiment is to see how great of a doctor you actually are. If you are great, then they should do just fine. They should all pass. If you are not, then they will fail. And, in essence, you will have failed at your job. Cause them to pass and you and they will live. Cause them to fail and you may not see many more days. But I did not lie when I said that you may leave here alive, as long as you follow my rules, but how long will you live in the outside world? You have built a life of secrecy. Your job requires you keep secrets. This is a difficult one to keep, but if you do not keep it you will be sent to prison only to live a sad and lonely life amongst the criminals. If you keep your secret, you will be saved from a life in prison, but you will be permanently scarred by what you have done. Can you live with that secret? Can your mind deal with that? If you're a good enough doctor then you won't even have to worry because everyone will have passed their experiments and they all will be set free. If you are not, then you will have failed. Once the experiments are over you have to call the police from your buddy's cell phone and tell them about the gunshots you heard as the neighbor. Make sure you tell them that your name is Jeffrey Thompson. And keep this letter as a constant reminder, if you want to try and prove your innocence it may be helpful. Good luck, Dr. Nickerson!

Chapter 49

Four experiments had already been completed and only three more stood in the way of the masked man. Only three more people that would be given the chance to succeed or fail.

Given the chance to live or die.

The man dragged Sara and Madison's dead bodies into the cellar and made sure the bloody mess upstairs was cleaned before getting the next participant.

The next victim.

* * *

"This shit is taking too long," Travis said. "I'm ready to get the hell out of here already. I mean, enough is enough."

"I agree with you. We've been locked in this room for almost two hours as it is and most likely one of us will be in here alone for at least twenty more minutes when he comes up to get the other," Kenny replied.

"So do you really think this whole experiment is to see how we behave in a stressful situation like this one? See if we get too scared and back down?" Travis questioned.

Kenny shrugged. "I'm not sure anymore. At first it seemed like it was, but then why would he be taking us all separately? That wouldn't be fair. We should be put into the same stressful situations."

"I just wish this was moving more quickly. I can manage being locked in this room if it gets me a friggin' 'A.' I'm not stressed at all. You must be stressing though," Travis responded.

Kenny looked confused. "Why do you say that?"

"Because you are afraid of closed places. Do you feel claustrophobic?" Travis asked.

Kenny laughed. "No. Claustrophobia isn't being afraid of closed places. I don't freak out when I go to a store and find out it's closed," Kenny joked. "Claustrophobia is fearing enclosed spaces. Like tight places."

"Same friggin' difference. Like elevators, and shit like that?" Travis asked.

"Yeah. I mean it's not too bad, it's not necessarily being put in small or cramped up places, it has more to do with the inability of getting out of those places. I mean, being in an elevator isn't too bad because I know it will open soon. Being cramped in the van on the way here I knew I could get out. Even though I'm stuck in this room I know I could get out if I wanted. But even if I couldn't, this room is too big to be afraid of being trapped inside. And every time someone leaves, it gets bigger," Kenny said.

"Well, I'm the next damn person to leave this room.

If he calls you next I'll pretend I'm you and bail," Travis replied.

Kenny thought about the idea. "I just thought about something."

"What is it?"

"We wrote down what we feared on the pieces of paper earlier and passed them back to the guy. I bet they have something to do with why he's taking us one by one," Kenny said. "We each have a different experiment that pertains to what we wrote on the paper."

"I'll certainly pass this then," Travis replied.

"Why do you say that? You're not afraid of having to do something with water?" Kenny questioned.

"First off, I'm not afraid of water. And secondly, even if I was, I didn't put that on the paper," Travis answered.

"You cheated?" Kenny asked as if astonished.

"No," Travis replied with a big grin. "I lied."

"What did you write?"

"I wrote…" Travis started to laugh, "I wrote that I was afraid of clowns. I saw on some show that there are actually a lot of people that fear clowns."

"I believe it. My brother was afraid of clowns when he was little. We had some weird painting of a clown in our room and he could have sworn that it was always looking at him," Kenny said.

"So if I have to do something with clowns I'm all set," Travis replied.

* * *

The masked man opened up the bedroom door and pointed directly at Travis.

Travis pointed to his chest. "Me?"

The man nodded. "Travis."

Travis walked closer to the masked man. "How did you know my name?"

The man shrugged. "Fifty-fifty." He motioned for Travis to follow him out the door.

Travis turned around and faced Kenny. "See you on the flip side, Ken. Time to go to the circus." He walked out the door.

The masked man shut the bedroom door and locked it.

"So what's my experiment?" Travis asked. "Anything worthwhile?"

The man didn't respond.

"So where are all the others?"

Still no response.

The man walked into the kitchen and started opening up drawers. Travis patted his back. "So what's my experiment?"

The man still didn't respond. He was busy fumbling through the drawers.

Travis removed his hand from the man's back and spun around to face the kitchen window. It was raining. The pitter-patter of the raindrops sounded peaceful.

"I thought it was going to snow tonight, not rain. You never know anymore. They say one thing and they mean another," Travis said as he turned back around.

The masked man pulled out three large knives from the drawer and placed them gently on the counter.

Travis smirked. "What are those for? You trying to scare me? You trying to pull one of those creepy masked guy routines where I'm supposed to think you're a killer or some shit like that?"

The man nodded.

Travis' smirk quickly became erased from his face. He let out a nervous laugh "Well, that may have worked for the girls, but not me. Stuff like that doesn't scare me."

The masked man put his hand in his pocket and pulled out a piece of paper. "Read this," he said as he handed it to Travis.

Travis looked down at the words on the sheet.

Experiment #5: The clown. So is it true that you're afraid of clowns or are you just joking? Perhaps you are just clowning around? I don't know if what you did was funny or not. If you are afraid of clowns then I suppose I don't have a great experiment for you, but that also doesn't mean I don't have one at all. But if you aren't afraid of clowns then I suppose this won't be funny at all. You won't be laughing once it's over. You won't be laughing once it's started for that matter.

Travis didn't finish reading. He looked back at the masked man. "What is this?" Travis asked.

The man reached into his pocket and pulled out the gun. "Do what it says."

Travis took a step back. "Whoa, man. What's going on here? What is all this?"

"You cannot be done that quickly," the masked man said.

Travis was confused. He didn't know what was going on. Was it more to scare him, more to test his stress?

Was the gun even real? he thought.

Travis shivered at the thought.

"Finish reading."

Travis looked back at the paper.

How are clowns scary? Is it the painted on red

grins they wear or the fact that they just don't look very kind? Even the happy ones seem evil for some reason. Let's test how much you truly fear them. I don't have a clever experiment having to do with clowns, but I figure they have jugglers at the circus and since clowns are in the circus I guess you'll have to juggle for me. The catch is you have to juggle three knives. Three sharp knives. If you can do it you'll live. If you cannot, then you'll be wearing red. It won't be paint though. Good luck!

"You can't be serious," Travis said nervously.

The man shook the gun at Travis. "Juggle and live."

"You are not for real. I can't juggle. I won't risk cutting myself with those knives," Travis responded.

"Do it and live. Don't and die." The man picked up one of the knives and held it out to Travis.

All that was happening bewildered Travis. *Was this really happening?* he thought. *Is this guy psychotic?* Travis stared at the gun in the masked man's hand. *Is it real?*

Travis began to shake as he noticed the red splotches on the man's jacket. *Blood.*

"Juggle," the man said as he shook the knife in his hand, wanting Travis to take it from him.

Travis reached out a trembling hand and took the knife from the masked man.

"Good," the man said as he reached over to grab a second knife from the counter.

As the man turned Travis stabbed the knife he held into the masked man's arm and ran towards the front door.

The man screamed in pain and pulled the knife from his arm. It dropped to the floor. The man ran after Travis.

He was about ten feet behind Travis when Travis turned the front door's knob. The gun was targeted at Travis' back. Just as the door opened a gunshot went off.

The bullet pierced just under Travis' left shoulder blade and hit his heart. He fell to the ground outside. Constant raindrops bombarded Travis' lifeless body. They kept falling down, wetting the ground below and washing away the blood that poured from his chest.

Eventually his dead body would lie in a deep puddle of water.

Chapter 50

When Boston police and detectives arrived at Nickerson's office they received a thorough report from Garrison and Billy. The two men didn't know much about the suicide scene themselves, but they made sure they told the police what they could. At first, Garrison wanted to get more FBI on the scene, but he figured he'd seen enough being there himself.

The crime was definitely just a suicide in his eyes. Nickerson was not a victim.

He was not murdered.

The suicide itself didn't puzzle Garrison, but the notes that were left did. Nickerson admitted his crimes. He was the one to kill the three people in the house, but more importantly he wasn't alone in doing it. He, too, was an experiment. Although he was the one who pulled the trigger, the crime was not his. The man who killed the three victims had killed himself, but there was something that was scary about the whole thing. The person who planned the murders was still out there somewhere. The true murderer was still alive.

He was still experimenting.

"So what do you suggest we do now? Still want to go to Miles' house?" Billy asked as he took his eyes off the road for a moment to glance over at Garrison.

"Well, first off, I suggest you turn the wipers on faster," Garrison said as he pulled the experiment paper from his pocket and looked at it.

"You took that with you? Isn't that tampering with evidence?" Billy asked in shock.

"That was a suicide back there. They don't need this. I left the article and I left the note he wrote. This is FBI business, I had to take it. There are clues in this that could lead us right back to the killer," Garrison replied.

"He *was* the killer, Hank. And perhaps it would have been better if you told the police you were taking that," Billy responded. "We could get into serious trouble."

Garrison ignored Billy's last two statements, but added to his first. "He was the one to do the killing, yes, but he wasn't the murderer. He wasn't the one to plan out the experiments. He was an experiment himself. The real psycho still exists."

"Maybe that's what he wants us to think. Maybe he wrote out that experiment letter so that we could think there was someone else," Billy said.

"Not a chance. Why would he do such an elaborate thing? The handwriting wasn't even the same on the two papers. He killed himself because he couldn't stand holding in the secret of what he'd done."

"Couldn't he have just told us without killing himself?" Billy asked.

"Not exactly. If he had, he still was the one to kill the people, and that would put him in prison. He said he didn't want to live like that," Garrison answered.

"Then why would he have kept the experiment note?"

"Either because he intended to try and prove his innocence or because he wanted us to find the criminal," Garrison said as he looked down at the crumpled up, stained paper. "He must have thrown it away at one point. He probably thought he had a chance to just forget about what he'd done and move on with his life. But even the experiment said it would be difficult. His thoughts overcame him and he had to get rid of them, even if that meant dying."

Billy nodded. "Just like the others. Their thoughts were too strong."

"That's right. Just like the others." Garrison flipped open his cell phone.

"Are you calling Miles?" Billy asked.

"Yeah. Head to his place."

Garrison closed the phone. "No answer." He looked back at the paper he held in his hand. "There's something important here."

Billy looked at Garrison. "Read it to me. Just the parts you think mean something."

"Every part means something," Garrison replied. "Experiment number four, the doctor…"

Billy interrupted. "Do you think the number four has something to do with the roses? In the video he mentioned that we have to find out what the roses meant."

"You may be on to something. At first we had no clue there were four experiments, but now we know there were. He had three real roses left near the dead victims, but his fourth was drawn. That may have been in reference to the fourth experiment, like you said." Garrison opened up the case folder and pulled out the transcript and read from it. "I'm sure you found my three roses among the wreckage. Let's make this number four. It's a rarity, you know. It won't happen again…you only get four. You have to figure out what that means."

"Why is it a rarity?" Billy asked.

"I have no idea," Garrison answered. "It's almost riddle-like. If the four roses had something to do with Nickerson, then why did he say it was a rarity? What does 'you only get four' mean? He goes on to say that 'only time will tell.' What the hell is this psycho's preoccupation with time?"

Billy shook his head. "I don't know. Maybe he's taunting us. Maybe he's telling us we only have so much time until he kills again."

Garrison raised his eyebrows. "Maybe we have no time at all."

Billy nodded. "Let's hope that's not the case. Read some more from Nickerson's experiment."

"Okay, this sounds interesting. Listen." Garrison read from the paper. "You have a simple task. All you have to do is see that the bulimic stays calm enough to finish her task with a gun aimed at her head. The tough part is that you'll be holding the gun. Then you must comfort your good friend, and patient, in the locked bathroom and try to have him pass his experiment. Then you have to wait with little miss sleepy head."

"What sounds so interesting to you?" Billy asked.

"It seems like whoever wrote this knew that Hartnett was a patient and a friend of Nickerson's. How could just anyone know that?" Garrison asked.

"True. Where would you even start to figure that out? Who would know about his patients? He told us they were all confidential."

Garrison nodded. "Not even his wife knew about them."

"So who could it have been then?" Billy asked.

"I'm not sure exactly. I suppose it's possible that it could be someone that knew the victim. Or even..." Garrison stopped.

"Or even who?" Billy asked.

"His secretary."

"That doesn't fit because the video clearly shows that beneath the mask was a man," Billy replied.

"I know that, but maybe it was someone she knew."

"If that were the case, we'd have to find out who she is and then find out about the people she knew. We don't even have an idea as to who she is. I can't recall her name. I know Nickerson said it a few times, but I don't remember it," Billy said. "Do you?"

Garrison shook his head. "No, I don't remember it either, but that's easy enough to find out." Garrison re-read what he just had. "You have a simple task. All you have to do is see that the bulimic stays calm enough to finish her task with a gun aimed at her head. The tough part is that you'll be holding the gun. Then you must comfort your good friend, and patient, in the locked bathroom and try to have him pass his experiment. Then you have to wait with little miss sleepy head." He stopped and rubbed his forehead. "Maybe I was jumping to conclusions."

"Why? What is it now? It still seems like he knew that Hartnett was Nickerson's patient," Billy replied.

"Yes, but he only knew Hartnett was. Nickerson's

secretary would have also of known the bulimic girl. He treated them both."

"So it's someone that knew only Hartnett, but not the other victims."

"Yes. Nickerson's secretary would have known the other victim was a patient of Nickerson's, she wouldn't of just known Hartnett," Garrison responded.

"But the secretary could have been new. Nickerson said he hadn't treated the bulimic victim for awhile," Billy said.

Garrison opened up his cell phone and dialed.

"Hello," a voice answered.

"Hey Arnie, it's Hank. I want you to find out what you can about Dr. Philip Nickerson's secretary."

"What's her name?" Arnie asked.

"We don't remember. That's where you come in."

"So you may be on to something?" Arnie asked.

"Hopefully. We figure that the·killer knew Nickerson and his patient, one of the victims," Garrison replied.

"Too bad the guy had to kill himself, huh? I mean, we'd be much closer to cracking this case if he had been around."

"I guess we'll never know," Garrison said.

"Okay, I'll see what I can do and I'll get back to you when I find something," Arnie replied.

"Yep."

Garrison closed the phone.

Billy looked at Garrison for a moment. "So what are we left with if she wasn't involved?"

"Pretty much anyone who knew Nickerson," Garrison answered. "And we can't count out Miles just yet."

"Read some more from the note," Billy said.

Garrison started to read more. "If they pass then you've done a job well done. You did what you studied to do and fixed them. If they fail you must shoot them…" He read some more silently before continuing. "The experiment is to see how great of a doctor you actually are. If you are great, then they should do fine. They should all pass. If you are not, then they will fail. And, in essence, you will have failed at your job. Cause them to pass and you and they will live. Cause them to fail and you may not see many more days."

"I hear 'passing' and 'failing' a lot in there. Is that all he talks about?" Billy asked.

"That seems to be the case. There's about ten times that either passing or failing is mentioned in here. I only know of one group of people in my life that used those words so much," Garrison said.

"Who would that be?"

Garrison opened up his phone before answering the question and dialed a number. "My teachers."

Chapter 51

The masked man grabbed at his wounded arm. The pain was almost unbearable, but he knew he was better off than the others. He inspected the stab wound and cringed at its deepness. Blood continuously poured from the gash and the flesh could be clearly seen, some hung out of the wound as if running away from the pain within. He took a deep breath and pulled out a piece of paper from his pocket and read it.

Experiment #6: The girl afraid of heights. What makes you fear heights? Is it that the higher you are, the longer the fall? Or perhaps it's because you don't feel secure enough when you get too high? Planes, skyscrapers, mountains, do they all make you cringe? Someone once told me that we are born with the fear of heights, for the unfortunate few they also must die with that fear. Here's your chance to finally get over the fear you've had since you were born. Here's your experiment. All you have to do is jump off the roof. It's only about thirty feet up, so at most you may break a leg, but it's better than dying. If you choose not to jump, then you fail and a bullet will penetrate through your skull. That way the fall will have no chance of killing you because the bullet already will have. It's a shot you have to take…or a shot I will take. Good luck!

In big letters across the paper was: *FAILED: SHOOT IN HEAD!*

The masked man shivered and put the paper back in his pocket. He walked down to the cellar and opened up the closet door.

Krista fell out.

She was still trying to wiggle free from the tape, but hadn't managed to do much. Her hands and feet were still securely taped together and the adhesive around her mouth still muffled her cries for help.

The man turned towards the bodies that lay on the floor before looking back at Krista.

Her eyes focused on the man's hand as he stuck it into his pocket and pulled out the gun. She shook her head in fear and closed her eyes.

"I'm sorry," the man said as he pulled the trigger.

Krista had no chance.

The man slowly bowed his head and picked up Krista's dead body. He pushed her back into the crowded closet, shut the door, and then began to walk upstairs.

His gun had one bullet left.

He had one experiment to finish.

And there was one victim waiting.

Chapter 52

"Still no answer," Garrison said as he shut his phone. "How much longer until we get there?"

"Probably around ten more minutes. Going to Nickerson's office backtracked us. It was completely in the opposite direction."

"I know that, it just seems like it's taking forever," Garrison replied. He looked back at the paper found in Nickerson's office.

"Do you really think Miles' did it? Before you said about how his office number was the same as the potential order of the victims' deaths, but now that theory doesn't work out. Nickerson was number four, so three-one-two-four doesn't make sense," Billy said.

"To be honest, Billy, I'm not sure who set up the experiments. Until we find out about Nickerson's secretary it's anybody's guess, but I do know that if Miles does know Nickerson we may have a breakthrough. Some of the stuff in Nickerson's experiment letter clearly point to the possibility of Miles," Garrison replied. "And we can only work with what we've got. Nickerson's wife said that Nickerson may have guest lectured at Bridgewater University and Miles is a professor there, so that part fits. Or at least that part could fit, depending upon whether or not Nickerson actually lectured there. But right now Miles is someone that fits the criteria, that's all I know for sure."

"But what about the other published ad? The one you showed me at the office. It was the same one that Nickerson had on his desk. They were conducted by Dr. Bert Over. He was trying to tell us something by leaving out the ad."

"Yes he was. I think he left the ad on his desk so that we could try and find the guy, but like I said to you before, those names aren't real. Bert Over could very well be Miles or Nickerson's secretary or someone else we may have overlooked. The names are just ways to throw us off. There was no Bert Over, we checked," Garrison said. "Just like there is no Frank Rose." Garrison looked at the other name he had written on the cover of the folder. "No Adam Johnson, or..." He turned to the experiment letter again. "Or Jeffrey Thompson. None of them exist. Not around here anyway. I'm sure someone had those names, just no one in the area, no one that could be part of this. And there's no way they were all involved, even if there were those people around here. This isn't some giant conspiracy. This is an experiment."

"Do you think the names have meaning somehow?" Billy asked.

"They could. Everything seems to have some sort of meaning." Garrison looked at the paper from Nickerson's desk. "He ordered Nickerson to refer to himself as Jeffrey Thompson when he called the police, so it must have some importance. But who knows anymore? He may just be leading us in circles."

Garrison closed the folder and added Jeffrey Thompson to the list of names on its cover.

"I don't understand how Nickerson could have murdered those people. I would just aim the gun at whoever ordered me to do it and kill that son of a bitch. Maybe he really *was* in on the whole thing," Billy said.

"I'm sure it sounds easy now," Garrison responded. "But think about it for a second. A guy has a gun to your head and orders you to kill other people or die yourself. By the time Nickerson could have spun around to fire a bullet at the murderer he would have been dead."

"And you don't think it's worth the try at least?"

"Not at first," Garrison answered.

"And why is that?" Billy asked.

"Because at first Nickerson may have hoped the victims would pass their experiments. If they had he wouldn't have had to kill them."

"Can you say you believe that? Can you honestly say that if they passed they would have been set free?" Billy questioned. "He could have still killed them."

"I'm sure he could have, but then he wouldn't have set Nickerson free. Nickerson passed, so he was let go. If he let one go then I bet he would have let the others go, too."

"Okay," Billy said. "So you didn't finish before, what about Nickerson trying to kill the murderer after he knew it was for real? After he had killed the first victim?"

"I'm not sure. I guess it boils down to the 'me or

217

you' type of deal. If you had a choice of killing yourself or someone else wouldn't you choose them?"

"That depends. I mean if it was me or someone I loved, I'd pick me," Billy replied.

"I know that, but Nickerson didn't love these people. He treated them, but they weren't people he loved."

"Doesn't that letter refer to one victim being his buddy? He must have been friends with him. He even went with him to the experiment. How could he kill a friend?" Billy asked.

"If it came down to it Billy, could you kill me?"

Billy didn't answer.

"Could you?" Garrison asked again.

"I don't know."

"Well, maybe you would know better if a gun was aimed at your head," Garrison replied. "We just don't know what we can do when a scary situation occurs."

Chapter 53

The masked man took a deep breath as he grabbed the bedroom doorknob. "It's almost done," he said. "It's almost done."

Kenny shot up from the bed as the door creaked open. "So last, but not least," he said. "Let's get this over with. I was getting lonely in here all by myself."

The man nodded.

"So how did everyone else do?" Kenny asked. "Did they pass or fail? How about Travis? What did you do with the clown thing?"

Kenny's questions went unanswered.

"Follow me," the man said.

Kenny walked right behind the masked man all the way to the cellar steps. The man stopped just before the first step and stepped to one side making room for Kenny.

"You first," he said pointing.

Kenny walked down the steps one at a time. As he got to one of the last steps he caught a glimpse of the two dead girls' bodies in the distance. The concrete floor was smeared in blood. Kenny was horrified and in shock. He turned to the man and his face dropped.

The masked man held out his gun, directly targeted at Kenny's forehead.

Kenny tried to say something, but nothing came out. His throat clenched up. He was all alone again. He and the masked man. The others had been murdered and Kenny realized that now.

No one could save him. He had nowhere to run to. His life quickly flashed before his eyes.

The man noticed Kenny's pained expression. "You can still live," he said. "They failed, but you can pass. You can live. Pass the experiment and you will survive. Trust me."

Kenny was trembling. "What experiment?"

The man held out a piece of paper.

Kenny shook his head, but didn't take it.

"Read this!" the man shouted.

Kenny slowly took the paper from the man's hand.

Experiment #7: The claustrophobic. Why are you afraid of enclosed spaces? Not enough room for you to move? Maybe it's because you feel trapped, like there's no way out. Maybe you feel stuck, caught with nowhere to go. Kind of like you must be feeling right now. Well this time there is a way out. This time you aren't entirely trapped. Your experiment is to be stuck in a cramped up closet. If you can manage to stay inside without screaming for help, or without trying desperately to get out, then you will have passed the experiment. Five minutes is all it takes. And don't worry, you won't be alone. Good luck!

Kenny looked up from the paper and at the masked man.

"Do it and live," the man said. "Do it and survive." The man pressed the gun to Kenny's forehead.

Kenny slowly took a step backwards down the last step. He was trembling with fear.

"Do it," the man repeated. "Open the door and get inside." The man pointed to the closet.

Kenny slowly turned the knob and opened up the door. Krista's dead body fell on top of Kenny.

Kenny grabbed her and screamed. "Oh my God! Krista!"

"Get inside! Get inside the closet!" the man ordered.

Kenny didn't hear him; he was too preoccupied with the body of his dead girlfriend. Kenny's eyes teared up. He was more in shock than ever before.

"Get inside the closet and live!" the man screamed.

Kenny still ignored the orders.

"Kenny, do it, please!"

Kenny didn't expect his name to be called out. It jarred him from his thoughts. Something seemed too familiar.

Kenny gently put Krista's body on the ground and then stood up. A tear rolled off his cheek. "Fuck you!" He screamed as he jumped onto the man.

The two fell to the concrete floor. Kenny grabbed at the man's hand trying to loosen his grip on the gun.

No chance.

The man held it with all his might. He would not be beat.

Kenny slammed the man's hand to the concrete floor.

He still held the gun.

He slammed it again.

And again.

Finally the gun was jarred from his grasp. Kenny went to grab it, but was pushed off the masked man.

The man reached for the gun and got a hold of it. He aimed it at Kenny who was just inches away. Kenny was like a madman. He didn't even focus on the gun and jumped right back on the man. Kenny only cared about killing the masked man; his thoughts didn't include being killed.

He was flipped over off the man. As soon as Kenny's back hit the concrete floor he bounced back up and went to attack again. He grabbed at the man's neck and began choking him.

The masked man flailed his arms at Kenny's back, fighting for air. He still gripped the gun, but hadn't shot it off yet. He pounded its handle on the back of Kenny's head.

Kenny ignored the pain and kept his hands around the man's neck.

Another blow hit Kenny's head. His grip weakened.

Another blow.

Even weaker.

A couple more blows to the back of Kenny's head until he finally stopped choking the man.

He gasped for some air and pushed Kenny's body off of him.

Kenny was in a daze, not yet knocked out, but headed there. He had no energy left. His fight was all for naught.

He tried one last attempt to kick the man, but it was useless.

He had lost the battle.

The man stood up and aimed the gun at Kenny, then shook his head. He picked Kenny up by the armpits and dragged him over to the closet. His whole body was limp. The man shoved Kenny inside the closet and shut the door.

The man waited outside the door.

One minute passed.

There were no noises.

Two minutes passed.

No cries for help.

Three minutes went by.

No screams from within.

Four minutes.

Silence.

Five minutes.

Kenny was either dead or too hurt to be afraid.

The man turned on the light and looked at one of the bodies lying across the room. "He passed," he said as he pulled off his mask.

Chapter 54

Billy pulled into Miles' driveway. "No one is here," he said.

"We'll wait," Garrison replied as he pulled open the folder. "Mr. Miles. Mr. Miles. Is it you that we're looking for?"

"What if he doesn't show up tonight? Are we going to wait here all night?" Billy asked.

"Maybe. I have a gut feeling this guy knows something. Maybe he's the murderer, maybe he's not, but so far there are many signs that point to him. If not him then we pretty much have to start from the drawing board again," Garrison answered.

"Well, we may have someone involved with the secretary," Billy replied.

"But until then it's Miles or no one. And 'no one' is a scary concept right now. 'No one' implies victory. And that victory chant will not be coming from our mouths," Garrison said.

"What more do we have to figure out? You say all the clues are within what we already have. What are we missing?" Billy questioned

Garrison pulled out the transcript. "One thing. One very important thing."

"What is it?"

"Remember how I said the times would be important?" Garrison asked.

"Yes."

"It's the one thing we haven't really figured out. Why put them there if they don't mean anything? They have to serve some purpose," Garrison said.

"What were they again?"

"The first victim had to last nineteen minutes and twenty-nine seconds, the second had to last nineteen hours and thirty-three minutes, and the third victim had to last thirty-two minutes. They all seem so unimportant and to me unimportant means important," Garrison said.

"Well, there was Nickerson, he was the fourth victim, he didn't have a time," Billy replied. "Why didn't he have one?"

"He did, in a way. Just not one like the others. His time was as long as it took for him to tell the police or kill himself. That didn't take too long. But we can't include him because he was just a prop being used in order to kill the others. We can't try to figure out what his intended time was."

"The other three times combined may mean something," Billy replied.

"Good assumption." Garrison looked at the times and added them up. "Twenty hours, twenty-four minutes, and twenty-nine seconds."

Billy thought of the numbers. "Doesn't seem to mean anything."

"No, it doesn't," Garrison agreed. "Twenty, twenty-four, twenty-nine. The second number is four more than the first and there were four victims. The third number is five more than the second, maybe he intends on killing five people this time." He sighed. "I honestly have no clue."

Billy scratched his head. "These riddles and numbers are killing me."

"And that's exactly what the killer wants them to be doing to us," Garrison added.

"Maybe the numbers are just completely arbitrary."

"They could be," Garrison said as he looked at the times. "But whoever could have thought out everything was smart enough to have a reason behind..." Garrison stopped as headlights shined through the car's back window.

"He's here," Billy said as the car pulled in beside his.

Miles rolled down his window and signaled for Billy to roll down his. Billy did.

"Are you looking for someone?" Miles asked.

"Yeah. Are you Mr. Miles?" Billy questioned as the cold raindrops spattered into his car.

"Yes."

"We're Agents William Boddicker and Hank Garrison of the FBI; can we come inside and ask you a few questions?" Billy asked.

Miles looked worried. "Yeah."

Billy nodded and rolled up the window. "Let's go," he said to Garrison.

Miles was at his front door when Garrison and Billy got out of the car. They ran quickly to Miles trying to avoid the raindrops.

Miles opened his door and wiped his feet on the mat before entering. "Awful night, huh?" he asked.

"Sure is," Garrison said as he and Billy walked into the house.

Miles closed the door. "So how can I help you?"

"We'd just like to ask you a few questions," Billy said.

"Can you tell me what this is about? It's not everyday that FBI is waiting outside someone's door," Miles said as he took off his jacket.

"That's certainly true, sir. We're working on a federal case right now that pertains to Bridgewater University," Garrison lied. "We've just been asking various people at the college questions that pertain to stuff that happened around here a few days ago."

"Oh, what sort of stuff?" Miles asked.

"We cannot reveal that information," Billy said.

"I'm sorry," Miles answered.

"So you are a professor at Bridgewater University, isn't that correct?" Garrison asked.

"Yes I am. Psychology professor, actually."

"That's good. How long have you been teaching there?" Garrison asked.

"This would be my fifteenth year," Miles answered.

"Do you do experiments there a lot?"

"It's funny you should ask that actually because my class has to do an experiment for me before Spring Break," Miles replied.

Garrison scratched his forehead. "Is that right? They have to do an experiment for you?"

"For me in the sense that it's for my class. I'm not conducting all the experiments. Does this have any relevance to what you're looking for?"

Garrison ignored the question. "What type of experiments do you do?"

"All kinds. The ones they could sign up for had to do with disorders or fears or varying types of moods." Billy looked at Garrison with wide eyes.

"Do you have a copy of the sign-up sheets?" Garrison asked.

"Not on me, sorry. I have some at the school, in my office."

"So your students sign up for experiments and they have to do them before Spring Break? When is Spring Break?" Garrison asked.

"Spring Break starts after classes on Friday. They have to do the experiment because I thought I'd be kind and not give them a midterm. The experiments are pass or fail; if they do them then they pass. They're simple."

Fail. Simple. Garrison thought. *Sounds like the video and Nickerson's note.*

"So who conducts these experiments? Professors?" Garrison asked.

"Mostly professors, but some students do them, too. I'm conducting two of them."

"Which ones?"

"One has to do with mood and the other one has to do with phobias."

Garrison remembered the ad from Nickerson's office. "What about eating disorders or anxiety disorders?"

"No. None have to do with that."

"Did you conduct an experiment on the twenty-sixth at the school?" Garrison asked.

Miles nodded. "Yes I did. It wasn't at the school though, nor was it for the school, just for my own knowledge. I'm writing an article on mood disorders and phobias so I needed to conduct an experiment to get data."

"Where did you hold the experiment?"

"In a Boston laboratory."

Nickerson worked in Boston, Garrison thought. "You wouldn't happen to know a Dr. Philip Nickerson, would you?"

Miles' expression remained unchanged. "Hhmmm, I can't say that I do. Should I?"

"I don't know. So are you sure you don't know him? Perhaps you met him on campus once as a guest lecturer? He conducts experiments, too," Garrison answered. He was just trying to read Miles' face to see if he caught him off guard with his questions.

Miles shook his head. "I would know him if he guest lectured there. The name certainly doesn't ring a bell. What did he guest lecture on?"

"Psychology," Garrison replied.

"If that's the case, I'm surprised I don't know him. I know everyone from the psychology department. If anyone guest lectures within the department it goes through all the professors, and that name doesn't sound familiar."

Garrison nodded. "Okay, what about a Dr. Bert Over or a Frank Rose?"

Miles shook his head again. "No. I'm sorry. I feel bad, you come here to ask me these questions and I don't even know the people you're asking about. I'm not very good with names though, so maybe I do know them, just not personally. Are these the people you are trying to find out more about? Are they part of the investigation?"

Garrison ignored the Miles' questions. "What do you do in your..." Garrison stopped as his cell phone vibrated on its belt clip. "Hold on just a moment."

"Hello," Garrison said as he opened the phone.

"Hey Hank, it's Victor. Where the hell are you?"

"In Bridgewater, why?"

"Oh good you're already there," Victor said.

Garrison was confused. "Already where? What are you talking about?"

"You don't know?"

"Don't know what?" Garrison asked.

"The Bridgewater police just got a call about ten minutes ago from someone in a rented out house near a pond. The caller said that there were five people murdered. He didn't know exactly where the site was, but said that it was about five to ten miles from Bridgewater University. The police are headed there now or at least where they think it is. They couldn't track down the call because it was from a cell phone. This could be the same guy as last time, but this time we have survivors."

"Where are the police headed?" Garrison asked.

"I'll find out and get back to you."

"Okay. Hurry up."

Garrison closed the phone.

"Who was that?" Billy asked.

"Victor Perrelli."

"Oh, the big guy. What was it about? Must have been important for him to call," Billy replied.

"I'll tell you in a bit."

Garrison turned his attention to Miles. "So where were you tonight?"

Miles was confused by Garrison's sudden change of questioning. "I was at a friend's house, why?"

"Where does your friend live? And who is this friend?"

"He lives about ten minutes away. His name is Henry." Miles looked bewildered.

"Henry what?" Garrison asked.

"Henry Dello. What is this about?" Miles asked.

Garrison ignored the question. "Is he a professor, too?"

"No. He's not."

"What were you doing there?"

"What? Why are you directing the questions at me? What did I do wrong here?" Miles questioned.

"What were you doing there?" Garrison repeated.

"I was invited over for dinner by him and his wife."

Garrison looked at his watch. "It's 9:40, seems like a late dinner."

"I went there early, had dinner, and stayed for drinks. What does this have to do with anything?"

Garrison's phone vibrated again. He flipped it open. "Yes."

"They figure the place is on Forsythia Lane. It's right near the college."

"Okay, I'll head there now."

Garrison closed the phone without saying 'bye.'

"So where is Forsythia Lane?" Garrison asked Miles.

"Um. It's about five miles from here actually. Just continue up this street and take a left at the end of it. Go about five miles down, it will be on your right," Miles answered.

"Okay, Mr. Miles, we may be back shortly so just sit tight," Garrison said as he turned the front door's knob.

Miles didn't answer.

The door opened and Garrison and Billy walked out

into the cold rain, ducking their heads down until they got into the car.

Garrison pulled out a pen and wrote something down on the front of the folder.

"What are you writing?" Billy asked.

"His license plate number, just in case we have to track him down."

"For what? Where are we going? How could we just leave a suspect's house?" Billy questioned.

"Forsythia Lane, Billy. Victor told me someone called from there reporting that five murders took place."

"Are you shitting me?"

"No," Garrison replied. "The call came about ten minutes ago."

"Then it's possible Miles could be the killer still," Billy replied.

"It's possible. But we can't assume this right now. He won't go anywhere as long as I have his information." Garrison looked down at the cover of the folder.

20FY24

"We should send some police to stay at his house until we know for sure. We don't want him to just get away if we found out some information that leads us back to him."

"I agree," Garrison said as he opened his cell phone and dialed a number.

"Yes, can you connect me to the Bridgewater Police Department?"

"Yes." The phone was directly connected.

"Bridgewater P.D., how may I help you?" a voice answered.

"Yes, hello. This is Agent Hank Garrison of the

FBI. I just wanted to request that a cruiser or two be sent to Randall Miles' house."

"What is the problem?"

"Nothing yet, but there could be. Just send some officers there until I get a chance to get there myself," Garrison answered.

"Okay. What is the address?" the voice asked.

"Twenty-nine Mary Lou Ave."

Chapter 55

Billy pulled into the muddy lane and stopped behind a few police cars and ambulances. "I wonder what sick and twisted experiment he pulled this time."

"Five dead, Billy. We were too damn late!" Garrison screamed. "That's a total of eight people that this sick bastard has killed so far. Eight people in a week. And we still have no clue what the hell is going on. This is not how it should be. This is not how I do things."

"But this time there were survivors. That could be very helpful," Billy said as he opened the car door.

The two men ran up to the front door, stopping right next to Travis' dead body. "Young kid," Garrison said. "He's targeting young kids now."

They stepped over the body and walked into the house. "Does anyone want to cover the dead body from the rain? Show a little respect, people. It's pouring outside," Garrison said angrily.

A couple of officers walked over to Garrison and Billy. "We weren't sure what we should do. We didn't

234

want to be tampering with evidence. This is obviously something greater than homicide so we didn't have jurisdiction," an officer said.

"You do now," Garrison replied. "Put some canvas over the body or something."

Garrison and Billy walked over to a suited man. "You a detective?" Garrison asked.

The man turned. "Yes I am. Who are you?"

"I'm Agent Hank Garrison of the FBI and this is Agent William Boddicker. How long have you been here?"

"About ten minutes," the detective replied.

"Where are the victims, other than the guy that's practically floating in rain water?"

"There are four dead bodies in the cellar," the detective said pointing down. "And the fifth is the one that was outside. All college students at Bridgewater University. Three girls and two guys."

"Where are the survivors?" Garrison asked.

"Upstairs right now. They're injured. Medics are working on them and trying to calm them down. One is a pretty badly beaten. Some head trauma. The other has a few bruises and cuts, one pretty bad one, too. Looked like he got into a fight with the guy who did this, he probably won," the detective said.

"Why do you say that?" Billy asked.

"He's still alive," the detective answered. "Neither one has spoken much."

"What are their names?" Garrison questioned. "The one with the head trauma is Kenny Paulson, the other is Perry Sinclair. That's all I know. They won't talk much. Too freaked out. Still too scared."

Garrison pointed to the steps. "They're up here?"

"Yes. Both are in two separate rooms."

Garrison walked up the steps and Billy followed behind. He pushed open a half shut door and walked inside. Kenny was sitting on the bed with some medics wrapping some gauze around his head.

"Hello. I'm Agent Hank Garrison. Can I ask you some questions?"

Kenny didn't respond.

"What's your name?"

Kenny looked at Garrison. "Kenny."

"What happened here tonight? Can you tell me what you know?"

Kenny shivered at the questions. He didn't respond.

"I know you've been through a lot tonight. I know you wish you could just forget about all that has happened here, but in order for us to find the one who did this to you and all these other people, we need your help," Garrison said. "Can you tell me what happened here tonight? Anything you can tell me would be helpful."

Kenny didn't respond.

"This is very important. We need your help with this investigation. What happened tonight?" Garrison asked.

Kenny's lips quivered. He wanted to speak.

"Go ahead, Kenny. Tell me what you can," Garrison said.

"Me..." Kenny took a breath. "Me and six other people...people from...from my school were brought here..." A tear started to form in Kenny's eyes.

"Okay, Kenny. Continue. You were brought here.

Who brought you here? What happened when you got here?"

"He...he was masked," Kenny stammered. "He picked us up at the college and brought us here. Then..." Kenny shivered. "Then he locked us in a bedroom and took us one by one."

"Didn't you think it was strange that he locked you in a bedroom? Couldn't you have called for help once you realized how strange it was?" Garrison questioned.

"He made us leave our phones. He said...he said it would cause too much outside interference. He said it was only an experiment."

"So you didn't think anything of it? Because it was an experiment you thought it was part of the study?" Garrison asked.

Kenny nodded. "I thought he just wanted to scare us. He even came into the room and told us it was to test our stress levels."

"And when he took each person out of the room you didn't hear any screams or gunshots or anything?"

Kenny cringed at the thought. "No. I didn't hear anything."

"What happened when he took you out of the room?" Garrison asked.

Kenny shivered. "He...he brought me down to the cellar. I...I saw the bodies...the dead bodies on the floor and freaked. Then he handed me a note and told me to do the experiment or die."

"He handed you a note?"

"Yes. It had my experiment on it. I had to stay locked in a closet."

"Why? Do you know why?"

"Because...because I am claustrophobic," Kenny

answered. "If I didn't last, I'd be killed. That's what it said."

"So you got into the closet? You lasted inside?" Garrison questioned.

"I...I didn't get into it. I was put in. I saw my girlfriend dead and I...I freaked out and attacked the man. I tried to get the gun from him, but he knocked me out with it. He put me in the closet."

"And you lasted, so he didn't kill you?"

"I think so," Kenny replied.

"And what happened when he let you out of the closet?" Garrison asked.

"I don't remember him getting me out of the closet. I...I think I was still unconscious."

"So, when you finally came to, what do you remember?"

"I remember seeing Perry, my friend Perry. He was looking at me. He was telling me to wake up. He said everything was going to be okay. He said everything was over. But it wasn't over. It wasn't over. People died. It will never be over. Never!" Kenny shouted.

"Calm down, Kenny. Calm down," Garrison said patting Kenny's shoulder. "How did Perry call the police if you said no one had a cell phone? How did he get one?"

Kenny shook his head. "I don't know. I didn't realize that. He just told me the police were on their way. That I was safe."

"Okay, Kenny, I'm through questioning you for now. Thank you for answering my questions. And you are safe right now. You are safe," Garrison said.

Kenny looked down and shook his head.

Garrison walked out of the first bedroom and into the second. He walked up to Perry, who was shaking on the bed.

"I'm Agent Hank Garrison. I'm here to find out who did this to you. Can you tell me what happened tonight?"

Perry was quiet.

"Did you call the police?"

Perry nodded.

"How did you call the police? Your friend Kenny told me you weren't allowed to have cell phones."

"We weren't. He gave me one after the experiment was over."

"Who? Who gave you one? Did you see who did this?"

"We all saw who did this," Perry replied.

Garrison was confused. "Did you see his face?"

Perry shook his head.

"Did he have a mask on?"

Perry nodded.

"Okay. Did you see him leave?"

Perry closed his eyes. "I saw everything," he said.

"You did? What did you see?"

"He brought us here," Perry took a breath. "He made us do experiments. We had to do experiments or die."

"What kinds of experiments?"

"Sick ones."

"Did he leave anything here? Anything that might be useful?" Garrison questioned.

"He left notes. He left his guns. He left everything."

"Where are the notes and guns?"

"In the cellar. In the closet," Perry answered.

Garrison was puzzled at how much information

Perry knew. "So you didn't see who did this to you? You didn't see his face? You have no idea?"

"I have an idea," Perry said shaking.

"Who? Who do you think?"

"I didn't see him, but when we…" he paused. "When we signed up for the experiment there were eight people."

"And?"

"And when we got picked up there were only seven people. Someone didn't show up."

"Who didn't show up? Who do you think did this?" Garrison questioned.

"Before we left I played basketball with some kid. His name was Fred. He's in the same class as me. The one we needed to do this for." Perry shook.

"You think he did this? You think he murdered these people, your friends?"

Perry shook his head.

"What do you mean then? Who murdered them?"

"I think he may have something to do with all this. He left before the experiment started. He just ran off, he looked scared. He could have been the other guy," Perry answered.

"Other guy? What other guy? Kenny is the other guy, right?"

"No. The guy that made me do my experiment," Perry said.

"What was your experiment?" Garrison asked.

Perry shivered, but didn't answer.

"You believe that this Fred kid is the murderer?"

Perry shook his head. "No. I know who killed the people. But he could have been the one… He was the only one missing."

"Perry, slow down. You aren't making sense. You said that Fred might have killed the people. But you also said you know who *did* kill them," Garrison said. "Which one is correct?"

"I know who killed them."

As soon as Perry answered the question Garrison's phone vibrated. He didn't check to see who it was and instead let it continue to vibrate on its clip. He was too wrapped up in Perry's questioning.

He was too close to finding out the answer he'd been looking for.

"Who, Perry? Who killed them? Did you see him?" Garrison asked.

Perry's eyes welled up. "I know who killed them. I know who pulled the trigger."

"Who? Who killed them? Tell me so I can help you," Garrison replied.

Perry put his hand in his pocket and pulled out two pieces of paper.

"I killed them," Perry whispered.

Chapter 56

Fred walked into his dorm room and sat on the bed. Troy was reading some history books at his desk.

"Where were you?" Troy asked.

"I was studying for a test in the library," Fred answered. "What did you do tonight?"

"Just read some more history books."

"How did History Club go?" Fred asked.

"Not bad. Same 'ol, same 'ol. It's kind of like history itself; you already know what is going to happen before it does. Did you have fun at your experiment?" Troy asked.

"Not really."

"What do you mean?"

"I don't know. We'll see how it goes tomorrow," Fred replied.

"Sometimes I don't get you, Fred. You just don't make sense sometimes," Troy said.

"Well, sometimes we never get anyone. I don't get you either most of the time. Sometimes you're sad, sometimes you're happy, but usually you're just reading about what happened in the past."

* * *

Miles sat across from two police officers. "So can you tell me what this is all about yet?"

The officers shook their heads.

"I don't understand all this. I come home to two FBI agents and then as soon as they leave you two appear. This is so strange. Did I do something wrong? What do you have on me?"

"We were ordered to come here," one officer said. "We have about just as much information as you do on this. We're both left in the dark, too."

"So cops just show up without reasons now, huh?" Miles asked.

"We have reason to be here."

"And what would that be?"

"FBI wants us here, so we're here. Simple as that. Do what they tell us. It's our job," the officer responded.

* * *

Garrison looked down at one of the papers Perry handed him.

Perry Sinclair
Afraid to die

He turned to the other one.

Experiment #1: The guy who's afraid to die. Tough thing to be afraid of since we all die at some point. What's life without death? Death is inevitable, so at some point you will be afraid to go. Maybe when you're old and gray. Maybe even today. You fit quite nicely into my experiments, I couldn't have planned it better myself. You have a choice that you must make. It is your experiment. You either pass or you fail. All you have to do is shoot whoever fails to follow their own experiment guidelines. Read them through so that you know what they are first. If they follow them, they will live. If they don't, they must die. If you fail to shoot them then you must die in their place. I know it may be difficult, but keep in mind that it's you or them. Who is more important? If you're afraid to die then the choice is rather easy, but if you are not afraid to die then maybe you're better off killing yourself instead of them. It's the only way to conquer your fear. Sadly it's the only way for you to pass your experiment- kill yourself or kill those that fail. Can you do it? If you would rather die then take the black gun from my hand, it holds a single bullet. Aim it at your head and pull the trigger. You will have died and perhaps in turn have saved your friends. Maybe not though. If you choose to live take the silver gun, it has six bullets. One for each failed attempt at the experiments. I suppose you could aim it at me, but I would bet against it. I'll be somewhere close by and if I even see the gun aimed in my general direction I'll shoot you first. It's easy. Put on the mask, it's eerily similar to my own, if you want to live. Disguise your voice. You will become me. You will be wearing what I have. You will be killing. Once you are done, hopefully with all six of your friends still alive, I will give you a cell phone and you can call whoever you want. Good luck!

Garrison was astonished. Perry had killed five people, but once again he wasn't the one to have done the experiment. It was just like Nickerson.

Garrison handed the papers to Billy. "Read these." He turned to Perry. "I know you didn't want to do this. I know it was life or death and you wanted to live, but you killed five people. You pulled the trigger. You have to be held accountable for it."

Perry nodded his head and began to cry. "I know. I didn't want to. I had to. I didn't want to."

Garrison walked out of the room and called over a few police officers. He whispered something to them and they walked into the room and handcuffed Perry.

They brought him out of the bedroom. He stopped in front of Garrison and looked up at him. "I'm sorry," Perry said in a whisper. "I'm sorry."

Garrison and Billy walked out of the room. "It doesn't seem fair," Billy said.

"What? Arresting that kid?"

"No, that the others all had a chance to escape death and he didn't. His choice was either kill himself to pass the experiment or kill the others who failed. Either way he'd end up where he didn't want to be. Behind bars or inside a casket," Billy replied.

"You're right; it doesn't seem fair now that you've mentioned it. Something isn't justified. Even the three other victims from before had a chance to live. So did Nickerson. Everyone but this kid could have passed without dying."

"Without dying or killing," Billy added.

"Well, actually Nickerson would have had a hard time. For him to live without having killed people he had to hope that everyone else passed," Garrison said. "But still, it does seem odd that this kid had no chance for a reasonable outcome."

. "Even Nickerson had some kind of hope. If he held the secret we may never have figured out he had something to do with it. That was his way out. Perry didn't have a way out."

The two men reached the cellar and looked at the four bodies lying on the floor. All with gunshot wounds to their heads. One with a missing eye.

"Sick son of a bitch!" Billy said. "That kid did all this?"

"I suppose we do things we don't want to when we fear them happening to ourselves," Garrison replied.

"It just seems a bit much to do out of fear. And even if he did it all to save himself he must be one sick bastard to have done all this in the first place. He also could have been lying. Maybe he did do this all. Maybe there wasn't another man," Billy said.

"That can't be. The other student, Kenny, said there were six others, besides himself, that were brought here. That means they were brought here by an eighth person. And Kenny didn't even know that Perry was the one to shoot the people," Garrison replied. "This mysterious eighth person devised all this."

"The two students both could have been in on it," Billy replied. "They both could have lied about there being an eighth person."

"It would be impossible. If that were the case, then they all would have walked here. Another person brought them here and that same person left them here after he was finished with them."

Billy nodded. "Everything is so odd. We have eight people murdered in a week and not one was killed by the hands of the guy we're looking for," Billy said.

Garrison shook his head. "I beg to differ. Although this guy didn't pull the triggers, he did kill those eight people. Hell, he even killed Nickerson."

Billy had nothing else to say. No matter what he could add would just be shot down by Garrison in the end anyhow.

Garrison turned to a man looking over one of the bodies. "Did you open the closet yet?"

"No, not yet. Still just looking at the damage done to the victims. All seem to be just a gunshot wound to the head, this one," the man said pointing to Madison, "had her eye ripped out and the guy upstairs had a wound to his chest. He must have been trying to escape. Too bad the poor kid was too late."

Garrison opened up the closet and looked inside. The folded up chairs and blankets were covered with blood. On the floor were a bunch of papers, two guns, and a black box. Garrison reached into his pocket and grabbed some latex gloves and put them on. He picked up the box and looked inside.

A mask.

He reached for the black gun. "This is the gun the note said had one bullet in it. Meant for that kid upstairs," Garrison said.

He opened up the chamber and looked inside.

It was empty.

"He could have lived," Garrison said as if in shock.

"How?" Billy asked.

"This gun had no bullets in it," Garrison replied.

"Maybe he used it."·

"Maybe, but maybe it was his way out. His way of passing the experiments. If he had pulled the trigger to kill himself he would have lived because no bullet would have come out. The whole experiment wouldn't have happened."

"There would still be a chance that whoever conducted the experiment would have gone through with the murders if Perry chose to pull the trigger on himself," Billy replied.

"Maybe. But we'll never know. Not until we find out who the hell did this." Garrison picked up the white pieces of paper.

He quickly read one.

"I can't believe this," Garrison said.

"What?" Billy asked.

Garrison handed him the note. "That one has to do with darkness."

Garrison looked at the next note. "This one must have been for Kenny, it's about claustrophobia." He flipped to another. "And this one has to do with heights. They all had to conquer their fears in order to survive."

"Yeah, that's what we were told before. We knew that already."

"I know. And remember what Miles said before?" Garrison asked.

"No, what?"

"He said he was conducting an experiment on phobias," Garrison said.

"So we're back to him again?" Billy asked.

"I believe we are," Garrison replied.

Garrison flipped through more of the notes and stopped at one that looked as if it had been written in blood.

The only thing to fear is fear itself.

Chapter 57

Troy put down one of his history books and looked at Fred. "Hey, I forgot to ask you, have you seen my razor blade?"

"Razor blade?" Fred asked. "No, why? Why do you even have a razor blade?"

"I like to cut out certain pictures in my books and paste them to my poster," Troy answered.

"You need a razor to do that? Haven't you heard of scissors?"

"The razor works better. Scissors can only cut out the pictures that are on the edge of the pages. The razor gets the more difficult ones, plus it allows me to cut out the odd-shaped ones quicker than scissors do." Troy pointed to his poster. "And most of the pictures I cut out are odd-shaped."

"Ugh," Fred replied as he looked at the poster of George Bush above Troy's bed. "Well, I haven't seen your razor. But that poster freaks me out. He always looks like he's watching me. It's like one of those pictures I used to have as a kid. The eyes always look like they are following you. Why do you have a picture of Bush above your bed anyway? Maybe one of his daughters, but not him. And why would you cut your textbooks up? You could sell them back to the school and make some money at the end of the semester."

"Nah. I like to keep my books," Troy replied. "They ease my worries."

"Well, whatever."

"Hey, another thing, Fred," Troy said.

"Yes," Fred answered, turning his attention from one of his own textbooks.

"What are you doing for Spring Break?"

"I'm not sure yet. Probably just relax back at home. Finally I'd have a chance not to worry about school work for a while."

"You could just not worry about it now. I mean, you don't even study and you never fail. You're like the smartest guy I know. I always wondered why you worry so much. You start to shake when you tell me about an upcoming test," Troy said.

"Let's not get into this. Didn't we already have this conversation last night? You get depressed at the drop of a hat and I don't make fun of you. If there's anything I worry about, it's not my tests, it's you," Fred replied.

"Funny. Well I wonder how you even did the experiment you had to do today. Do you think you passed or failed?" Troy asked.

"Both."

* * *

Miles heard a knock at his door and went to answer it. He opened it up and saw Garrison and Billy outside.

"Oh, it's you two again. How can I help you now? There's already a bit of a police party happening inside. Can you please tell me what this is all about?" Miles asked.

"Sure. But first can you tell me if there was an experiment being done today for your class?" Garrison asked as he made his way inside.

Miles' face looked surprised. "Yes, there was actually."

"Who was conducting it? Were you?"

"No, I wasn't part of it. I don't even know who was. I don't remember if it said so or not. Like I told you before, the experiments are at the school. I don't have any with me," Miles answered.

Garrison didn't buy it. "So you're telling me you didn't conduct an experiment tonight?"

Miles nodded. "Yes. That's what I'm saying."

"And you have no idea who may have held today's experiment?"

"None whatsoever. I know I am conducting two, but I really haven't talked with any of the other professors, so I'm not sure. Plus, it could have been a student."

Student, Garrison thought. *Was Miles telling the truth? Did he really have nothing to do with the murders? Was it a student of Miles' that made it seem like Miles was the murderer? The kid did say something about someone not arriving to the experiment. Fred.* "Do you have a Fred in your class?"

"I'm awful with names." Miles thought for a moment. "Fred. Fred. Fred. Yes. I think I do. He's a smart student. Always answering questions."

"Smart, huh?" Garrison asked. *Smart enough to set up the experiments.*

"Yes. Hold on a second while I get my class roster just to make sure. I could be thinking of the wrong kid. Fred, Phil, Frank, they all sound familiar," Miles said as he turned around.

Frank, Garrison thought. *Frank Rose.* "I thought you didn't know a Frank," Garrison said.

Miles turned back to Garrison. "I don't. I was just using those names because they all kind of sound the same, Fred and Frank. I don't think I have a Frank in my class. But I'll check for you on that one, too."

"I'll go with you," Garrison replied.

The two men walked into a bedroom and Miles grabbed a bag off his desk. He took out some folders and placed them on the top of his desk. He opened up the one marked *Abnormal Psychology MWF.*

Miles opened up the folder and pulled out a long sheet of paper. He scanned the list. "Right here," he said pointing to a name on the list. "His name is Fredrick Tout. He's a senior and a psychology major."

Garrison looked at the class roster. "Does he live on campus?"

"It wouldn't say here. I'm not sure. Maybe. I think I even remember seeing his name on the experiment…"

Garrison interrupted. "So first you tell me you don't know if there's a Fred in your class and then you tell me you remember seeing his name on the list? That seems a bit odd. Your memory comes and goes, now doesn't it?"

Miles was confused. "I honestly wasn't sure if I had a Fred in my class, but I remember now that I see it written down. You know how seeing things in writing brings back memories?"

Garrison knew he was right. He had to look at the

video's transcript numerous times. He remembered better with written, rather than spoken, English.

"Okay. So you have no clue if he lives on campus then?"

"Well, the experiment was tonight at seven o'clock, so he probably does."

"What do you mean, 'probably'?"

"Well, unless he lives really close by, coming to campus for a seven o'clock experiment would be difficult," Miles answered.

"Who would know for sure?"

"The registrar's office, but it's too late. They won't be there."

"How about on the computer?" Garrison asked looking at Miles' desktop computer.

"Actually, yes. I can go online and check the Bridgewater class directory. If he lives there it should say. Now can you please just tell me what this is all about? The whole situation is kind of scary."

"Indeed it is, Mr. Miles. Indeed it is," Garrison replied.

"So I have no chance to get you to tell me, huh?" Miles asked as he turned on the computer.

"Not yet. Hurry up and find me the kid's address."

"It takes time," Miles answered.

Time, Garrison thought. *Time.*

Chapter 58

"When do you think you'll be going to sleep?" Fred asked Troy as he turned out his nearby light.

"Soon, probably," Troy replied.

"Soon? You always say 'soon,' but you never sleep. When was the last time you actually slept? I don't know how you do it."

"I get my fair share. It's like they say, 'you can sleep when you're dead.'"

"I'd rather sleep while I'm alive, thank you very much." Fred rolled over onto his stomach and placed his head on the pillow. "Goodnight, Troy."

"Goodnight."

Troy quietly ripped out a page from one of his textbooks and folded it up. He picked up a container of glue and smeared the paper's corners with the sticky substance then walked over to the poster above his bed and glued the paper beside Bush's mouth.

"Perfect," he whispered.

Troy walked back over to his desk and within seconds an array of emotion soon swallowed him up. He quickly sat in his chair and bowed his head, shaking it from side to side. His eyes were welling up. Sadness had started to overcome him.

His depression was taking control.

He shut his eyes tightly and massaged his temples in an effort to release the strain he was feeling.

It wasn't working.

He pulled open a textbook and tried to read. It usually worked.

Not this time.

More and more burden seemed to pile on top of him. It was eating him up inside.

He needed to fight it. But he only knew of one way. He pulled up his sleeves and looked down at his cut up arms. It was as if his skin was calling out to be cut. It *needed* to be cut.

He pulled back down his sleeves and shook his head.

Troy's head was screaming at him. It was calling for his help. He needed to please its cries. He closed his eyes, but it was no use. He needed to cut.

He *needed* the razor blade.

He opened his drawers, but to no avail. *Fred took it,* he thought. *He was lying. He knows where it is.*

Troy walked over to Fred's desk. He slowly opened up the first drawer and looked inside.

Just school papers and essays. No razor.

He opened up a second drawer and looked inside.

More papers. All papers about fear. Still no razor.

Troy opened up the last drawer. Fred rolled over and squinted at Troy. "What are you doing?"

Troy was silent.

Fred sat up. "Troy, what's wrong? What are you looking for?"

Troy remained silent. He just stared at the contents of the drawer.

On top of a pair of black gloves lay the razor.

* * *

Miles and Garrison stared at the computer screen.
Fredrick Tout
Senior
Dakota Hall
Room 112

"There you go," Miles said.

"Good," Garrison replied as he wrote down the hall name and the room number inside the cover of his folder. He closed the folder and then added Fred's name to the bottom of a list that already filled the folder's cover; Frank Rose, Randall Miles, Bert Over, Adam Johnson, and Jeffrey Thompson were the others. "Call up your friend that you told me you were with tonight." Garrison had to make sure Miles' alibi stood up, if not he had a false lead.

"What?"

"Call him up. I would like to speak with him," Garrison replied.

"Why?"

"Just call him up, Mr. Miles," Garrison ordered.

Miles walked over to his nightstand and picked up his phone. He dialed a number.

"Hello," a groggy voice picked up.

"Hi Henry, it's Randy. Sorry to call so late."

256

"Is there a problem, Randy?" Henry asked.

"No." Miles covered the phone and turned to Garrison. "Do you want to talk to him?"

"Yes," Garrison replied.

Miles talked back into the phone. "There's someone from the FBI here."

"What? Are you in some sort of trouble?" Henry asked.

"No. He would like to speak with you."

"Are you serious, Randy? What is this all about?" Henry questioned.

"I'm not sure myself. Just talk to him." Miles handed the phone over to Garrison.

"Hey, Henry, this is Agent Hank Garrison from the FBI. I just wanted to ask you a few questions."

"Oh, no problem, sir," Henry said, his attitude had changed.

"What were you doing tonight?"

"I was with my wife and Randy. We watched a movie and had dinner," Henry answered.

"What time was that at," Garrison asked trying to see if it fit with Miles' own alibi.

"He came here at seven. I think he left about and hour and a half ago."

"Okay, Henry. That's all I wanted to know. Thank you very much and have yourself a goodnight."

"You too," Henry replied as the phone hung up.

Garrison handed the phone back over to Miles. "Here you go."

"What is this all about? Can you tell me that? Can you tell me what this is all about?" Miles asked.

Garrison shook his head and rubbed in between his eyes. "You'll find out soon."

Garrison walked out of the bedroom and over to Billy and the other two officers. "Billy, let's go. We are headed to Bridgewater University to meet with a Fredrick Tout."

One of the officers stood up. "What do you suggest we do? Should we stay here?"

Garrison thought for a moment. He wasn't too sure about his lead. *If it was the student, then how did he know about Hartnett being Nickerson's patient and friend? Why would a student know that?* "Yes," Garrison finally said.

Miles was stunned. "I don't understand. What more could you want from me?"

Garrison didn't answer. He opened up the front door and walked outside. Billy followed.

"So what is going on?" Billy asked as he backed out of the driveway.

"Miles has an alibi. He was at his friend's house when the murders took place. It may not have been him," Garrison replied.

"But you still aren't sure? Is that why you still have the police posted there?" Billy questioned.

"No, I'm not sure. He could have planned that I would call his friend to see if his alibi checked out. He could have told his friend to lie," Garrison said.

"So he's still a suspect then?" Billy asked.

"Yes," Garrison answered. "But right now we have to go to Bridgewater University."

"Don't you think that if Miles was a cold-blooded murderer he'd just find a way to take down those two cops?" Billy asked.

"Maybe, but I doubt it."

"You doubt it?"

"Seems like the real killer doesn't like to do things without help," Garrison replied.

Billy turned to Garrison and immediately was drawn to the cell phone on Garrison's belt. "Hank, your phone keeps flashing."

Garrison looked at his cell phone. "Oh yeah. Arnie called while we were back at the crime scene. He must have left a message. I was too wrapped up in the survivors at the time that I forgot about it."

"It must be about the secretary."

Garrison nodded. "He took forever to get back to me." He opened up the phone and pressed a button. It automatically dialed his voicemail.

'Hey, it's Arnie. I don't know what you're doing right now, but I found out some stuff about the doctor's secretary. I'm sorry it took awhile, but it was difficult working without a name. Her name is Alaina Dello...'

Garrison hung up the phone and turned to Billy. "Turn around."

Billy was confused. "What now?"

"The secretary's last name is Dello," Garrison replied.

"That sounds familiar."

"It should. It's the same name as the guy Miles told us he was with tonight," Garrison said.

Billy was stunned. "So it really may be Miles, huh? He could have gotten the information from the secretary because she's his friend's wife."

"That's what I'm thinking. It would make perfect sense. I don't even know why I suspected the student. He wouldn't have known Nickerson."

"So what are we going to do?" Billy asked.

"We're going to make them tell us the truth," Garrison answered.

"Them?"

"Yes. We're going to go to this Alaina Dello's house and see what they have to say about all this. That way there will be no more chances for Miles and his buddy to talk about fake alibis," Garrison said.

"What?"

"Miles thinks we're headed to the college, but we're not. If the alibi truly doesn't check out then we've caught them," Garrison replied. "There's no way their alibis can be airtight if they committed the murders. There would be no time for them to have discussed what they were going to say. I asked his friend over the phone what they did tonight and he matched up with what Miles said, but that was one question. There might not be such a perfect match when I start asking multiple questions."

"I'm so confused right now. I thought the whole thing was that this guy would go easily if caught. If it really is Miles, how come he was making it seem like he was oblivious to the whole situation?"

"I can't sit here and tell you that I'm certain Miles is the murderer, or even that the secretary has some sort of connection to this, but I will tell you that if it were the case it would make sense. I know the video said something about 'going easy if caught,' but I'm not so sure the person that did this really wanted to get caught," Garrison answered.

"So where am I headed?"

Garrison opened his cell phone. "Just head straight for now. I'll find out where the house is." He dialed up Arnie.

"Hey Arnie, it's Hank again."

"You get my message?" Arnie asked.

"Yeah, can you quickly tell me where this Alaina girl lives?"

"I told you in the message. You just said you got it," Arnie said.

"Yeah, I didn't get to listen to it all. Where does she live?" Garrison asked again.

"Um…hold on while I find the paper…okay she lives at forty Gifford Road."

"Great. Thank you."

Garrison hung up the phone without a 'goodbye.'

"Turn at Gifford Road. It should be close by. At least if Miles was telling the truth about that," Garrison said.

"It would seem weird to be telling the truth about that if he's the murderer," Billy replied. "I mean, if he lied about everything else, why tell the truth about this?"

Garrison didn't know how to answer the question. Billy was right. "Turn here," Garrison said pointing to a street.

Billy made a right turn down the road. "What number?"

"Forty," Garrison replied.

"Here it is then," Billy said turning into the driveway of a small blue house.

Garrison opened the car door. "Remember they're just suspects right now. They aren't criminals. We're here to ask questions and see if they can be answered correctly. We're here to see if the alibi fits. We don't have enough evidence just yet to pin the murders on them."

Billy opened his door. "Whatever you say."

***

Fred got out of his bed and walked over to Troy. He put his arm around Troy's shoulder. "What's wrong, buddy?" Fred looked down at the drawer and closed it.

"You lied," Troy said.

"About what?" Fred asked.

"You said you didn't take my razor blade." He pointed to the closed drawer. "But you did. I saw it in there. You did take it. You lied to me."

Fred ignored Troy's remarks. "Troy, just calm down. I didn't lie to you. Just calm down. What is it that makes you sad all the time? Can you tell me that?"

Troy shook his head. "I don't know."

"Take some deep breaths, Troy. Everything will be fine. You're just a little stressed out, that's all. I get stressed out sometimes, too. Sometimes I do stupid things when I'm stressed," Fred said. "Things I regret having done. Don't make the same mistake I have and go through with them."

Troy took a few deep breaths. He was becoming calmer.

"Sit down," Fred said as he gently pushed Troy to his bed. "You'll be okay."

Troy nodded.

Fred picked up one of the history books from off the ground and handed it to Troy. "Read this. It's what you like to do when you're sad, right? Trust me, Troy, this feeling will pass. A couple of minutes are all it takes and it will pass. Just last a couple of minutes. Trust me, Troy. You have nothing to fear."

***

Both men stood outside of the front door. The rain poured hard down on them. Garrison rang the doorbell.

The door opened just moments later.

Alaina stood inside the house.

"Oh, hello guys. So we meet again. Come inside. It must be freezing out there."

The men walked inside. Alaina closed the door.

"So what brings you here? Is there a problem?" Alaina asked.

Garrison ignored the questioning. "Where's your husband?"

"What? Why?"

"Where is he?" Garrison repeated.

Alaina didn't understand why they wanted to speak with him. "He went to bed awhile ago. Would you like me to wake him for you?"

Garrison looked around the house. He saw some wine glasses sitting on a large dining room table with some Chinese food containers by their sides. "You have a party tonight?"

Alaina smiled. "No. I wouldn't call it that. My husband had a friend of his over for dinner."

"You usually leave it out like this after you're finished eating?"

Alaina glanced at the table. "Oh, I'm sorry for the mess. I was actually just about to clean up. I was caught up in some crime show on television though. I got sidetracked."

"You like crime, Mrs. Dello?"

"What? I don't understand. Can I ask you what you are getting at?" Alaina asked.

Garrison didn't answer. "Do you ever hang out with your employer, Dr. Nickerson?"

Alaina shook her head. "No. Why?"

Garrison would not answer. "Do you happen to know a Frank Rose?"

"No."

"How about a Dr. Bert Over?"

Alaina shook her head. "No."

Garrison looked down at the cover of his wet folder. "How about Adam Johnson? Jeffrey Thompson? Fredrick Tout?" Garrison shook his head. He had read too far. Fred's name wasn't fake. "Nevermind the last one."

"Nevermind Fredrick?" Alaina asked.

"Yeah. Do you know the other ones I mentioned?" Garrison asked.

"No," Alaina replied. "But I do know Fredrick."

Garrison looked at Billy then turned back to Alaina. "How do you know him?" Garrison asked.

"He's a patient of Dr. Nickerson's."

Garrison was shocked. *That explains how he knew Hartnett was a patient of Nickerson's. He was one, too,* he thought. *Miles wasn't lying. The student does fit. It all makes sense now.*

"How long has he been going to Dr. Nickerson's?"

"Just under a year," Alaina answered.

So that's why he wouldn't have known the bulimic victim. She hasn't been a patient of Nickerson's for a while, Garrison thought.

"Why does he go to Dr. Nickerson?"

"He suffers from panic attacks."

"How bad are his attacks? Do they cause him to do stuff he necessarily wouldn't?" Garrison questioned.

"I don't know. I'm not sure how bad they are or what causes them. I only know that Dr. Nickerson is treating him for anxiety. I'm sure Dr. Nickerson could answer these questions better than I could."

Garrison didn't respond. He knew Nickerson would not be able to answer the questions. Nickerson was dead.

"Do you know when the last time Fredrick came in for an appointment?" Garrison asked. "Did you see him at the office at all today?"

Alaina shook her head. "He had an appointment today, but he never showed up. As a matter a fact, I think his appointment was set for around the time you showed up at the office today."

He was probably planning out the whole experiment at that time, Garrison thought. "What time was that?"

"His appointment was for three o'clock. He hadn't missed one before today. It was odd because he never fails to show up."

He will now, Garrison thought.

"Okay, well thank you for your time. I'm sorry to have bothered you, Mrs. Dello," Garrison said. He turned to Billy.

"Let's go."

***

"So what do we have now?" Billy asked. "Is this it

or will there be another abrupt 'turn around' speech sometime soon?"

Garrison was agitated, both at Billy's questions and at himself. He doubted his own ability. It was as if he didn't even pass his own experiment. He failed with finding the killer before he struck again and then he failed numerous times afterward with pointing out suspects that weren't suspects at all. Garrison was upset.

"How do we even know for sure that it's this student?" Billy asked. "I thought you said whoever committed the murders would have to know Hartnett was a patient of Nickerson's. How would this kid know that? Isn't there confidentiality?"

"He never referred to Hartnett by name. He only mentioned that he was Nickerson's patient. He probably saw the guy at Nickerson's office while he was there himself. They probably even waited in the waiting room together at some point. Either way he knew he was a patient of Nickerson's and that means this kid fits every criteria possible," Garrison answered.

Billy nodded.

Garrison opened up the folder and pulled out Nickerson's note. "Listen to this," he began, "Experiment number four, the doctor. So you told some of your patients this would be a good study for them to join. Like the nice doctor you are, you even came along with one of them."

Billy didn't understand. "What about it?"

"It's like I should have seen this all sooner. It pointed to a patient all along."

"What?" Billy asked. "Why do you say that?"

"The part that says, 'like the nice doctor you are'," Garrison answered.

"And?"

"Well, it seems to imply a patient. Someone that went to Nickerson for help. Someone that considered him to be kind," Garrison said. "Someone that thought of him as a 'nice doctor.'"

"Many people could have referred to Nickerson as a 'nice doctor.' His secretary, his friends, his wife."

Garrison smiled. "Billy, do you know any doctors?"

"Yes."

"Do you know doctors that you don't go to? Doctors that aren't personally your doctor? Ones that don't treat you if you're sick?" Garrison questioned.

Billy didn't know where Garrison was going with his questions. "Yeah I do. My wife's friend is a doctor and I never go to him. Why do you ask?"

"Because you can't refer to a doctor you don't go to as a 'good' doctor. You don't know how good of a physician someone is unless you have had them as a doctor," Garrison replied. "I know plenty of doctors and I can't tell you if they're nice doctors or not. I can tell you if they're nice people, but unless I'm their patient I cannot tell you how great of a doctor they are."

Billy nodded. "Okay, that makes sense. But even still, you think that one sentence in that note should have pointed us to the student awhile ago?" Billy asked.

"Not really, but it's there. We never knew this Fred kid was a patient of Nickerson's, but now that we do, it makes sense. I'm just upset it took so long."

"It's not anyone's fault. Earlier everything pointed to someone else. Nothing ever pointed to a student," Billy replied.

"But then again it all did," Garrison said. "I just wasn't smart enough to see it." He shook his head. "I can't believe I wasn't smart enough to see it. I failed at my own job. I failed at the one thing I do well."

"You can't say everything pointed to this kid. You can't kick yourself because we made some mistakes," Billy replied. "The only reason we got this far is because of you. Who knows where we might have been without all you've done. We didn't fail. You didn't fail."

Garrison shook his head. "Think about all I've missed. The kid from the house said that one student didn't come to the experiment. That student is Fredrick Tout. Come to find out he's a psychology major. Miles said he is a smart kid. He also said that some students conduct experiments," Garrison responded. "And to top it all off, he's a patient of Nickerson's."

"But the only reason we know all that now is because of all the work we've done. Look at everyone else, Hank. They're all just sitting around scratching their heads. Hell, I would be doing the same thing if not for you."

"It's just funny how everything suddenly comes together now. It's funny how I see how this Fred kid fits it all," Garrison said. "He's smart, he's a psychology major, and students can conduct experiments. He lives on campus, which is just a few miles from the site. If he did this he could have just left after the experiments were done and drove home." Garrison paused. "Shit! *Drove* home."

"What?"

"He obviously drove the victims to the site and drove back. I never asked the survivors if they knew what kind of car the masked man drove."

"What good would that do? Do you think it might be someone other than this psychology student now?" Billy questioned.

"It's not that. It's just that tracing the car could have ended all this. Shit! It was so easy and it was right in front of my face."

"We can call and find out from the men at the crime scene what he was driving. Maybe they asked," Billy said. "But isn't the student the prime suspect now anyhow?"

"I think so. But then again where has that gotten me so far today?"

Garrison flipped open his cell phone and dialed a number.

"Victor, it's Hank. Who is at the crime scene right now?"

"Well, shit, Hank, you should be there."

"I was. I was just getting a head start on things. I know you've heard that one of the living people was the one to kill the others."

"Yes I did. But I also heard that he wasn't the guy to set up the whole thing," Victor replied.

"No, he wasn't. That's what Billy and I were doing. We thought we had a lead and went to go check it out," Garrison said.

"Hank, you can't do this all the time. You're supposed to notify me when you do stuff like this. I tell you where to go and what to do. You know that."

"It just didn't cross my mind. I thought I had something. Who's at the scene now?" Garrison asked.

"What do you think you have?"

"Fredrick Tout may have done this. He may have been the one to set up the experiments," Garrison answered.

"Who is Fredrick Tout?"

"He's a student at Bridgewater University."

"A student, Hank? You think a student did this?"

"All signs right now point to him. There's no one else," Garrison responded. "So we're headed to see him now, but I need to know who is at the scene from FBI to see if they could tell me what kind of car the person was driving. If we know that, we can trace it back to the killer. There's still the possibility that it's not who I think it is. The car would assure me if I'm right or not."

"It seems like other people are doing there jobs correctly, Hank. You can't always try to be the savior. You can't always jump to conclusions," Victor said.

"Who is there so I can call them and find out what I need to know?"

"You don't need to call them. Unlike you, they called me. The guy was driving a white van. The students didn't know the license plate number so we really can't trace it yet. We're having people look at vans that are owned in the area, but I don't recall there being a Fredrick Tout who owned one," Victor said.

"It was probably rented then. Did you check to see if any were rented?"

"Yes. We did. Just one from the area turned out. It was rented today at three o'clock."

Same time Fredrick had the appointment he didn't show up to, Garrison thought. "Who rented it?"

"Do you really think that matters? You know by now that the names are all fake," Victor replied.

"To who?" Garrison asked again.

"To a Mr. Clint Williams. Does that mean anything to you?" Victor asked.

"Not to me, but to someone it does."

Chapter 59

'Bang. Bang. Bang.'

Fred's eyes quickly darted towards the door. "Now what is it?" he asked.

Troy shut his textbook and got up from his bed. "I'll get it."

He opened up the door. Garrison and Billy were outside, dripping wet.

"Are you Fredrick Tout?" Garrison asked.

Fred heard his name and quickly got up off his bed.

"No," Troy answered. "I'm his roommate. He's inside though."

"We're Agents Hank Garrison and William Boddicker of the FBI, could we come in?"

Troy nodded his head and opened the door wider, inviting them inside.

"You wouldn't mind waiting outside or going somewhere else while we talk to your roommate, now would you?" Garrison asked Troy.

"No, not at all," Troy answered.

"Okay. It shouldn't take very long."

"I'll just be outside," Troy replied as he closed the door.

Garrison and Billy walked into the room and saw Fred sitting on his bed. "You're Fredrick Tout, right?' Garrison asked.

Fred nodded. "Yes. What is this about?"

The question was ignored. "Where were you tonight?" Garrison asked.

"I was in the library," Fred answered nervously.

"Are you sure you want to tell us that? You sure you went to the library?"

"Yes. I was studying for midterms," Fred replied.

"I heard that you were supposed to do an experiment tonight. Did you do it?"

"No. I didn't. I signed up for it, but I didn't go," Fred replied.

"Oh, you didn't? And why is that?" Garrison asked.

"I just didn't go. I didn't want to do it."

"Fredrick, I would be completely honest with us if I were you. Right now you are a suspect in a crime. If you are lying to us you will be jeopardizing yourself. Did you go to an experiment today?"

Fred was scared. "A crime?"

Garrison nodded. "Did you go?"

"No. What kind of crime?" Fred asked trembling.

Garrison didn't answer. "Why didn't you go?"

"My doctor told me not to," Fred answered.

"Your doctor?" Garrison was interested.

"My psychiatrist."

"Psychiatrist?" Garrison asked, wanting more.

"Yes. Dr. Nickerson. I go to him…."

Garrison interrupted Fred. "Dr. Nickerson?"

"Yes. Why? Do you know him?"

"Yes I do," Garrison answered. *It all makes sense. He matches up so far.* "Why do you go to him?"

"I go to him for my panic attacks. What is this about?"

"Dr. Nickerson told you not to go to the experiment?" Garrison's head was flooded with ideas. *Did Fred really not go to the experiment? Was he telling the truth? Did Nickerson really know who the killer was? Was he protecting Fred from taking part in an experiment he knew was deadly?*

"He didn't tell me not to go to it, but he told me to experiment with my attacks."

"Experiment? What does that mean?" Garrison asked. *Was Fred just lying to protect himself? Was he really the murderer? Maybe Nickerson didn't commit suicide after all. Maybe he was murdered because he knew too much.*

"Dr. Nickerson told me to fail at something." Fred was trembling uncontrollably now. "He told me if I failed at something I would know what it felt like to fail. Does this help you at all? Is this what you're looking for?"

Garrison didn't understand. "So you didn't go to the experiment tonight because he told you to try and fail something?"

"Yes. He never told me to intentionally fail at something, but that it may help me if I just failed and saw that it didn't matter. I was going to go to the experiment, but I ended up just going to the library because I thought it was something I could fail at. The grade was pass or fail. If I didn't do it I would have failed. I would have failed at something. So I didn't go. And I didn't feel that bad afterwards. He was right. He didn't tell me what to do, but he helped me either way. Does this have to do with Dr. Nickerson?"

"So you are afraid of failure?" Garrison asked. *Just like me,* he thought.

"I guess so. And the only way I can get rid of that fear is if I conquered it. That's what he told me," Fred answered.

"So you didn't go to the experiment tonight because of that?"

"Yes."

Garrison wasn't sure what to believe any longer. His mind flipped from thinking it was Fred to believing what Fred was saying and thinking someone else was a part of the whole experiment. *Someone out there is the killer,* he thought. *If not Fred or Miles or Nickerson, then who?*

Soon his head was being bombarded with unanswerable questions.

It could be still be Miles, he thought. *Shit, I was too anxious in getting here that I forgot to be more thorough. I forgot to look for signs.* He shook his head and began to rub his forehead. He was becoming pale.

Billy grabbed Garrison's shoulder. "Are you okay?"

Garrison didn't answer. Numbers flashed into his head. *Twenty, twenty-four, twenty-nine. Those were the combined times.* He looked down at his wet folder. In running black ink he saw *20FY24.* "It's Miles, Billy. It's not this kid. It's Miles."

Billy was confused. "Miles checked out, Hank, you know that. He had an alibi, remember? That's why we're here."

"Twenty and twenty-four are the numbers on his

license plate." He handed Billy the folder. "And his house number is twenty-nine."

"It's just coincidence," Billy replied. He was finally fed up with Garrison's over-analytical theories. "Numbers are everywhere. I mean, look around." He glanced over the room. "Look at that Chinese food, that could be a number twenty combination plate."

Garrison didn't pay any attention to Billy. "Yeah."

Billy glanced over the room further. The Bush poster caught his eye. "Look, right there, at the poster; president forty-three, right? And all the others, presidents one through forty-three. What about those numbers? And why are we using those combined times instead of the original times? Why? We even said earlier that combining them may mean nothing."

"You're right; we should be using the original numbers." Garrison looked at the poster. He remembered the amount of time the bulimic victim's experiment was supposed to last. "Which president was number thirty-two?"

Billy shrugged. "I don't know, Truman? Hoover?"

"Roosevelt," Fred chimed in.

"Roosevelt," Garrison repeated. "This isn't your poster, is it?"

"No, it's my roommate's."

"Does your roommate like presidents?" Garrison asked walking closer to the poster.

"Loves them. Anything to do with history, I guess. It seems like it's the only thing that makes him happy. Seems like lately he's had a bout of depression," Fred answered. "Why do you ask?"

"Just wondering," Garrison said as he looked at the pasted on cutouts that graced the poster.

He stared at the cutout of Franklin Roosevelt. *Frank Rose,* he thought. *That's where he got the name.*

Garrison nodded his head. *Franklin Roosevelt. It would never happen again.* He thought of the video. *The four flowers must have symbolized his four presidential terms. That would never happen again.* He looked at the other men that adorned the poster and thought about the other fake names. *Dr. Bert Over was Herbert Hoover. Adam Johnson was John Adams. Jeffrey Thompson was Thomas Jefferson. Clint Williams was Bill Clinton.* Pictures of those presidents decorated the poster.

Garrison squinted at the words beside Bush's mouth.

The only thing to fear is fear itself.

Garrison looked at the other words glued to the poster.

I will be remembered, not forgotten. I am not worthless. I am victorious. History will remember me.

Garrison turned to Billy. "Get the roommate in here now!"

Billy nodded his head, but was puzzled at Garrison's sudden request. He walked over to the door.

Garrison shook his head and glanced down at one of the history books atop Troy's bed. He opened it up to a bookmarked page.

1929-1933

Billy opened up the door.

Garrison remembered the times the other two

victims had been given in order to survive. *Time,* he thought. *Nineteen minutes and twenty-nine seconds. Nineteen hours and thirty-three minutes. Nineteen Twenty-Nine to Nineteen Thirty-Three.* He looked at the title on the page.

The Great Depression.

Enjoy other great titles by David DeMello:

Speak No
Evil

David DeMello

CPSIA information can be obtained
at www.ICGtesting.com
Printed in the USA
BVHW040842010522
635492BV00002B/224